How Do You Plead?

by
Mark Mayes

xulon
PRESS

One

"**M**atthew Craig you have it all", he thought to himself. "Another day, another 50K", was his motto and his religion at his high-stakes, high-tension job in the Big Apple, New York City. A very successful attorney at the prestigious law firm of Steele, Gold, and Rich; a licensed broker, but only to dabble in as a hobby, and for some "very special acquaintances"; he considered himself too busy and too guarded to have friends. His work is his friend. He knew he could always count on it being there. The events of 9/11 forever changed his outlook. The people that he considered friends, the only people he ever cared for and loved, other than his family, were lost on that tragic morning. Those events caused Matthew to put his faith and his Bible on a shelf where they would not be in the way; the one event caused Matthew to become the hard-hearted man he is today.

"Be a success today; don't waste time worrying about tomorrow's consequences until they materialize, if they do", Matthew thought. After all, he may not need to worry about it, anyway; he could die tomorrow just as thousands did back then. If he was going to become the success that he moved to New York to become, he had to become heartless, and never allow his feelings to dictate his life. "They cannot make me a success; they cannot make me rich", he remembered himself saying the day after the tragedy. Get rich today, spend it today, if you can. "After all, I worked hard for it, so I should spend it as I see fit! Why leave it for someone else to enjoy?" Matthew thought to himself often. "After all it is my money!" Oh, but do not let his frivolity mislead you – Matthew has made sure that his retirement will be "golden". He could retire tomorrow and never have another care in the world, but he continues to accumulate. His theory is that he should be able to live daily after retirement as he does now, without any compromises or sacrifices.

He was working during the day, and socializing at night. This is how you meet your next client – rubbing elbows with the high society and the wannabes. The contacts you make, the women you date; it is all part of the lifestyle, it is all part of the game. Every night it was a different party, every party a different woman- no commitments, no regrets. Some thought that it had become his mission statement. He follows it religiously and rigorously. Matthew also spends an hour daily in the health club that is located on the ground floor of his building. Many wonder how he finds an hour each day in his schedule to allow this, but in the same breath, they will tell you it is obvious that he somehow does. His stamina is among the elite few, and his physique would make even the most stringent body builder envious. It is true that 'the image makes the man', and Matthew is doing everything he can to insure he is the man that fits the image!

Matthew lives in one of the most glamorous suites available in Manhattan. He could watch some of the most majestic sunsets, if he was home to enjoy them. He owns <u>cars</u>, which is normal for most people, but in New York, where the preferred mode of transportation is either a taxi or the subway, he is in an exclusive club. Just the rent for parking spaces would pay for most people's apartment rent for a year. He has a car for every occasion. He has his Ferrari to hit the roads to unwind and to think, and to satisfy his need for speed. He has his Bentley Continental GTC for his "date car". He has his Hummer to satisfy his need to be an off-road, four-wheeling kind of man. His final piece of the collection is his "work" car. Are you going to take clients to lunch? Are you going to an important meeting? Do you have a big day in court? Take the trip in style! How many people do you know in New York own a Maybach? How many people own a Maybach, period?

He has a wardrobe to match every occasion and every vehicle. His bank account is bigger than his reputation. He has it all. Simply put, he is "the man!" Women want him, and men want to be him.

Tonight he is going to a VIP dinner at the Omega Hotel. The Omega, constructed in 1886, considered the most elite hotel in New York, the first hotel in New York to cater to the desires of the rich, affluent, influential, important people in New York. The architecture of the Omega is even more majestic than the list of dignitaries who have stayed there. Two white ivory pillars that were hand crafted in Africa and shipped here by boat adorn the massive foyer at the entrance. The intricate carvings on the pillars are a reflection of the landscape of Africa as well as New York. As many people have commented, "from one jungle to another!" The murals that cover the ceilings are a thing of beauty; depicting the rich and vast history of the great city the Omega has been a part of for over 100 years. The gold leaves that adorn each section of the murals glisten from the light from the magnificent crystal chandeliers that hang just off from the welcoming and registration areas. The floors are of the highest quality marble ever seen. When you walk on it once, you will never forget the distinct sound that your shoes make on this floor. Egyptian lace covering padded velvet walls are what await you in the elevators, with gold handrails to lean on or hold on to as you make your way to your destination. The "rooms" resemble a small apartment or a studio than a hotel room. There is even a telephone in the bathroom, which by the way has a Jacuzzi as well. If this does not do the trick, just call the main desk and they will send up a masseuse to help you relax and unwind from all the stress of the day.

The dinner hall, The Upper Room, is extraordinary, and the food is impeccable, with only five-star chefs working in their kitchen. You can experience all of the luxuries that the Upper Room has to offer from the comfort of your room if you prefer. As is the case many times, if you are incapacitated and unable to enjoy the elegance and atmosphere of this impeccable dining room, or if you just simply require a certain level of privacy, you can go the conventional room service route and have it prepared in the kitchen and delivered to your room immediately. The heated silver delivery carts assure you that it will arrive as hot as it would at your table if you were in the dining room.

The transformation of the ballroom of the Omega into its state of dress tonight is something most people only see in their dreams. The ballroom, Secrets, is as big as a football field; the walls are a very relaxing burgundy and gray combination of colors, the floor is cherry wood, but tonight there were several Persian rugs lining the floor to dampen the noise from the dancers. The ceilings constructed with the same crystal chandeliers and murals. The stage area is in the center of the ballroom, which allowed for optimum sound, and access to and by all parties was equal. There was a bar at either end of the room, of course, as it is all about convenience. There are tables in discreet areas that do not interfere with either the stage or the dance floor, but still allow access to the bars. The lights are at a minimum, allowing for privacy, for those moments of 'secrets'.

The party- invitation only- called the "Alpha New York", if you are at this party, you are somebody! Since the invitations were limited to 100, this had to be the best of the best! The movers, the shakers, and the moneymakers; these are the ones that got it done at all costs! To be fair, there was a sprinkle of those on this list that had done outstanding charitable and philanthropic work as well. People will do *anything* to be a companion to one of the invitees, and anything to stay a part of this lifestyle. For Matthew, this party is not about whom he was going to meet, but who was going to have the opportunity to meet him! This is his night! This is his night to play and party hard! That is his work tonight, already neatly organized as his Palm Pilot. If everything goes according to plan (and it usually does), he would leave the party by 1:00 AM, be home with one of New York's most lovely women by 2:00 AM, get to sleep by 4:00 AM, and end his power nap at 7:00AM, and be in the office at 9:00 AM. After all, it will be Sunday morning, so there is no reason to be at the office at 7:00 AM on a Sunday. His itinerary has him making calls to Tokyo, Chicago, and Miami. After that, he was going to check the research results on his computer, take off to pick up some lunch, then head home to watch the game. This is the first game he will be watching on his new 70" plasma HD television. After all, would visitors expect anything less? He IS Matthew Craig!

As he arrives at the party, the valets are scrambling to get the opportunity to park Mr. Craig's Ferrari. This will be the only opportunity that they may ever get to sit in such an automobile. His date for tonight, Miss Nicole Banks had used her good looks to get her out of Billings, Montana, and into New York City, but not anywhere else significant since arriving three years ago. She had heard about Matthew through some of her girlfriends at the agency. Their stories were all the same; arrive and enter the function with Matthew, be introduced to some of the elite while together, and then you were free to do whatever you wish until the end of the event, or until Matthew was ready to leave. Yes, it is a fact that you were going home with him that night, and sex was usually the finality. You may even get a second opportunity to go out, but those were rare. Overall, all of the women agreed that the contacts made at these parties and events to elevate your career and your status far outweighed a little meaningless sexual pleasure. Besides, it's only sex, not a commitment, and everyone knew that Matthew was not ever going to marry, and almost every woman agreed that they were not going to give up their career dream for any man at this point, as your window of opportunity is small. As for Matthew, he was already scoping out the room as they entered the ballroom, looking for his next paycheck.

His eyes told him everything he needed to know about a person; he was an expert at reading body language. Once he knew your silent, unspoken, and your true thoughts and feelings, he knew how to approach you and present himself so that you were completely confident that it was you that approached him when the conversation was over. "I'm so good, it's a crime," Matthew would often say.

Many of the faces were familiar, but not all of them were. There were several possibilities. He was always up for any challenge. "Oh, well, same old, same old," Matthew thought to himself as he escorted Nicole into the room. He will find out soon that he is so very wrong!

His companion, Ms. Banks, had already excused herself to the bar. She had been told by several of her friends that you will usually find your next paycheck at the bar, and at the very least, your next opportunity to attend the next big gala. As for Matthew, he was still scoping the room; he did not need a drink, but he got one just to have the glass in his hand.

As he turned away from the bar, he noticed a stunning young woman sitting at a table near the stage. She looked as if there was a light focused on her; she was radiant; she was quite possibly the most beautiful woman he had ever seen!

She was not wearing any of the designer dresses that all of the other women were wearing; her dress was just a plain, but very tasteful, black evening gown. The lights from the stage also allowed him to see that she was wearing a beautiful pearl necklace, and earrings to match. This woman was elegance; she was total class, and Matthew thought to himself, "This woman is very impressive!" He could not ignore her over-whelming presence; she had an aura about her, a glow if you will, and it was not because of her perfectly tanned skin; he could not quite figure it out right at this moment, but he had to know more about her. As only Matthew could do, he confidently walked over to her table, ready to begin his inquiry.

"Good evening, I'm Matthew Craig," he said as he extended his hand.

She reached out to shake his hand as she answered, "I know. Everyone knows who you are."

Matthew replied, "Well, that's not entirely true. I did not catch your name"-

"That's because I never told you," she replied. "You see, unlike you, I do not come to these parties to draw attention to myself. I only do it because my work needs all the publicity it can get, and that means that I have to be here."

A woman of mystery! Matthew was enjoying this! "Let me try again. Good evening! My name is Matthew Craig; I am an attorney. I have not had the privilege of meeting you! What is it that brings you to this party?" he inquired of her.

"Good evening, Mr. Craig, I'm Elizabeth Angel. I am the Chairperson for the non-profit group D.I.E.T. that is currently raising funds to build new churches and schools as well as help feed the hungry children in Ethiopia and Uganda," she replied confidently.

"Oh, so you are here to try to solicit some big bucks from the big shots," Matthew questioned. "What does that stand for? I do not think that a diet is what they need! More likely, it is food that they need!"

"D.I.E.T. is an abbreviation for 'Delivering Internal and Eternal Transformations'. No, actually, I'm being recognized for the money that I was able to collect this year, but if you would like to contribute, I would be more than happy to take some money off your hands, or anyone else that would consider it. It would allow us to get to Zimbabwe much quicker than we anticipate!" she replied.

Matthew answered, smiling, "Call me at my office and we can make an appointment to discuss a donation. Here is my card. You said that you are receiving recognition for your work! Just what did you accomplish this past year, Miss Angel? Angel, ha, I bet that gets the donors nervous!"

"Please, call me Elizabeth, and yes, it did cause me to get a few chuckles as well as a few negative responses. People thought that I was using my name in an irresponsible and some even said unethical way to gather contributions! However, after a few minutes, I was able to put them at ease and convince them it was not about me, but it was about the children and the families that are suffering and needing our help! And by the way," she closed in saying, "I was able to collect over forty million dollars this year for our outreach!"

Matthew gasped, "Forty million? Wow! I am impressed! You can do a lot of living on a four million dollar salary. You *do* get 10% do you not?"

Elizabeth looked at him quizzically and replied, "No, I do not have a four million dollar salary. My salary is the same each year whether I raise one million or 100 million dollars. I am satisfied with my earnings. I'm not rich, but I have no needs, and my bills are paid."

"That is not a way to negotiate a salary! I can find you a place in my foundation that will pay you 10%, and with your fundraising skills, you would make millions easily!"

Matthew explained. "Let me have one of your business cards! With the commitment, dedication, and desire you have shown to D.I.E.T., your future can only be brighter! And if I may add, much more lucrative, as well!"

Elizabeth responded, "You will never understand. As I said before, it is not about me! I am doing this for the people that will probably never have all the opportunities that I have been blessed to have in my life! I do not need lots of money to be happy. That huge salary that you would pay me could be doing more work for the foundation! I am too busy to spend it, and even if I did have it, I would donate most of it! Besides, I don't need the temptation from the money to lead me somewhere or to something that would cause the need for me to confess to my Father later."

"You are old enough to not have to have your Dad's permission or approval for everything! Wait-you do not still live at home, do you? Can't you afford an apartment in New York?" Matthew asked. "Like I said, you can use 10%!"

"No, I don't live at home, thank you; I happen to have a very nice penthouse in one of the historical landmarks in the city! It is quite spacious and has a lovely view from the balcony to enjoy the sunrises! One of our largest benefactors owns the building, and the studio was a storage facility for his offices. When he had learned of my plight in finding an apartment, he offered the penthouse to me at the rent controlled rates everyone else in the building was paying! I had never met the man, but because of my work, he was lead to help me! Besides, in this city, we're practically neighbors! Moreover, you are right, I am a big girl, and I do not ask my parents for permission for everything. They know that I listen to the instructions from my Heavenly Father, so they know that their prayers for Him to give me wisdom are all they need to say."

Matthew groaned, "Oh, I should have realized sooner. You are one of those 'religious 'people!"

Two

Elizabeth responded quickly, "No, I'm not one of those 'religious people'! Religion is what is destroying the churches and the world today! I hate religion! Did you know that Jesus hated it, too?"

Matthew was speechless for a moment! This was like the opposing attorney presenting undisclosed evidence in a trial! He had to regroup without letting her see any loss of composure, just like in the courtroom. "Elizabeth was absolutely stunning!" Matthew thought to himself. She is <u>real,</u> unlike all of the other women that he has been acquainted with over the past six years! "She is so easy to talk to, and she does not seem to even care about my money!" She reminded him of a time and place when he was much more trusting, caring, loving; before the world changed and made him become the cold unfeeling person he is today. He was unable to read her, as he was anyone else he knew. She was very open, approachable, but had a presence surrounding her, as if it was illuminating her obviously radiant beauty, yet shielding her, as if to say, "Back off!" Matthew looked up to see if he could find Nicole in the room. Of course, just as he thought, she had surrounded herself with some heavyweights and their dates. "She is succeeding just as I presumed! She is chatting with some of her girlfriends, and meeting some of their dates! She does not miss me! Besides, I'm not done with this conversation by any means!" Matthew thought to himself.

"Matthew, what's wrong? Are you trying to find a legal answer to the question?" Elizabeth asked, laughingly. His silence had surprised her.

"I'm sorry, Elizabeth. I was just somewhere else for a moment – I really do-

Elizabeth interrupted, "I'm sorry. You need to be some-where else. I understand. I am sure you are missing your date. I noticed you looking for her. She is very lovely. I'm used to being at these things alone. It's okay. It was nice to meet you, Mr. Matthew Craig!"

Matthew quickly rebutted, "I was not excusing myself! No, I was not looking for my date; her name is Nicole Banks, by the way, well, I was looking for her, but to make sure that she was busy, as I knew she would be. I am not trying to find a polite exit from you! Your response merely caught me by surprise! I thought that Jesus was the reason for religion! When I was growing up back home, I do remember that the preacher was talking about God or Jesus every week! As an attorney, I need to hear your evidence that Jesus hates religion!"

"Why don't you review the evidence that you already have, counsel?" Elizabeth asked. "What do you remember from your years of attending church when you were younger?"

"There is not much to remember, really. It has been a while." Matthew admitted, "What exactly are you trying to prove?"

"Only that you remember more than you realize. Do you remember when the Pharisees became upset in Matthew chapter 12 because the disciples picked corn to eat, and then again when Jesus healed the man who had a withered hand?"

"Not really," Matthew admitted.

Elizabeth continued, "They said that it was unlawful to do these things. And Jesus explained to them that they were condemning Him and the disciples for gathering food, and they did nothing to David when he ate the food of the priests; and then he asked them if a sheep that has fallen into a pit on the Sabbath, would they not rescue it? Jesus was showing them that they were enforcing the *letter* of the law. But the *purpose* of the law was to worship God on the Sabbath, as the commandments declared. The Pharisees were not being loving and understanding. They expected others to follow the laws, but they had reasons as to why *they* were exempt from these same laws. Legalization poisons a church by following *the letter of the law, and not the purpose of the law.* In the gospel of John, in chapter 5, Jesus healed a man that had been lame for 38 years, and then in chapter 9, He heals a man that had been born blind. Both of these miracles performed on the Sabbath. This made the 'religious' leaders enraged, as Jesus had broken their laws of doing works on the Sabbath. The hardness of their hearts could not allow them to see the lives that were changed or the praise that these people were giving to God, they were too busy proclaiming a broken law!"

"But without rules, there would be no boundaries or order within the church!" Matthew rebutted. "I am sure that Jesus requires order within the church!"

"You are right, He does! But if we did not allow healing to take place on the Sabbath, how many do you think would receive their healing? If we did not lay hands on the sick in our churches on Sundays today how would we heal the masses?" Elizabeth asked.

"I think it would be safe to assume not as many," Matthew replied. "You are right; I stand corrected. How can you remember all of this? Like I said, even though I went quite often when I was younger, I really cannot recall anything that I was taught!"

Do you remember John 3:16?" Elizabeth asked.

"Uh, oh, wait a minute, that's the one about God's only son and eternal life, right?" Matthew responded.

"Close, but not quite," answered Elizabeth. "It says 'For God so loved the world that he gave His only begotten Son. That whosoever believeth in Him shall not perish, but have everlasting life.'"

"That's what I said!" Matthew exclaimed.

"No, it wasn't!" Elizabeth snapped back authoritatively. "You can't just add or delete words to fit in your own little box!"

"But you know what I meant!" Matthew pleaded.

Elizabeth responded to his frustration by asking, "What if you were in a courtroom and you had a client charged with murder. Would you make a statement like, 'My client is innocent because he was not at the murder scene,' or would you say, 'My client is innocent due to the facts entered into evidence, that stipulate that he was seen by several people at Joe's Restaurant, and we have over 10 sworn statements and signed affidavits that attest to this fact.'

"Well, that's easy, the latter statement, of course!"

Matthew answered. "By the way, that was pretty good! What are you not telling me about yourself?"

"Stop changing the subject!" Elizabeth answered quickly.

"Why did you choose the last statement?"

"Because that statement explains all the facts in detail and clarity with no room for interpretation." Matthew answered.

"Well, the Bible is the same way! You have to have all the facts and all the details. It is a matter of life and death as well!" Elizabeth explained.

"I've never heard of anyone being put to death because somebody left a word out of a Bible verse!" Matthew rebutted.

"I'm not talking about the physical body being put to death! I'm talking about the spiritual death!" Elizabeth pleaded.

"Oh, okay, so you play the fear card when you raise your money! I knew there was something that you done! You cannot win over everyone by being beautiful all the time!" Matthew answered as if he had just settled a huge litigation.

"No! I never bring up my faith and my beliefs unless they open that door first, and then I politely but confidently walk in." Elizabeth proudly responded.

"More like you storm in!" Matthew chuckled.

"That's not my style. You are good at changing the subject! Let's get back to you! What else can you remember from your days in church?" Elizabeth asked again.

"I told you, not a lot really; I do remember our preacher always warning us kids to 'always be on guard 'cause the devil is just a'waitin' to trip you up!' He would tell us that 'the devil ain't in the beer joints on Saturday night, he's in the homes of the Christians!' Matthew recalled. "What do you think of that? I mean, Satan was in the bars, too, right?"

"I'm sure he was, or at least his demons were. But more than likely, that statement, to some degree, is true!" Elizabeth replied.

"Wait a minute! So you are saying that Satan has angels? I know of Hell's Angels, and I've even represented a group of them before - you know - the biker gang? But I thought that angels were from Heaven?" asked Matthew.

"There are both Heavenly and demonic angels. Do you remember the verse that tells us this fact? In Matthew 25:41, Jesus said, 'Then shall he say also unto them on the left hand, Depart from me, ye cursed, into everlasting fire, prepared for the devil and his angels:' So now you have evidence, counsel!" Elizabeth explained.

"So hell IS for the devil!" Matthew exclaimed.

"Yes, it is, but it is also for anyone that does not believe or disobeys the words of the Bible and does not accept Jesus Christ as their Lord and Savior!" Elizabeth continued.

"But I believe in Jesus and Heaven and hell, so I'll go to Heaven, right?" Matthew asked.

"Matthew, even the devil believes in Heaven and hell, and he knows Jesus on a personal level, but that will not get him any closer to Heaven! And to answer your question, no, you will not, unless you have repented of your sins and asked Jesus to come into your heart! Romans 3:23 states, 'For all have sinned, and come short of the glory of God.' Elizabeth answered. "As an attorney you would agree that all means everyone? It didn't say almost everyone or most or many; it said ALL!"

Matthew shrugged slightly but noticeably and replied, "That would be correct."

"But don't get discouraged, Matthew, for in the very next verse it says, 'Being justified freely by His grace through the redemption that is in Christ Jesus.' and Romans 6:23 reminds us, 'For the wages of sin is death, but the gift of God is eternal life through Jesus Christ our Lord.' How would you sum up your life to this point, Matthew?"

"I don't know! I guess it has been okay, I mean, like everyone else, it's had its share of trials and heartaches, and it's had its moments of satisfaction and happiness as well. I guess I am better off than most, as I have everything that I need, and if I want something, I have the resources to just go buy it. I have a very comfortable place to live, I'm in good health; I would say that I am very fortunate." Matthew reflected. "And I guess I've been lucky, as well."

"How do you mean?" Elizabeth asked.

"Well, at the top of the list for the foreseeable future, was a court appointment that was moved up a day due to a last minute settlement, and since my case was next on the docket, I was the beneficiary." Matthew somberly stated.

"Well, for someone who considers that to be lucky, you didn't sound too happy", Elizabeth observed.

Matthew paused, and then proceeded to elaborate. "That day was September 11, 2001. I would have been there meeting with a potential client that morning if the courthouse had not called me to appear there, so I cancelled my appointment, and went to appear in court. Shortly after all parties were assembled, we were dismissed due to the attacks."

Elizabeth took a sip of her iced tea, then responded, "You know what some people consider luck, other people see as divine intervention."

"I don't buy that! Why wasn't there 'divine intervention' for the people in the towers? What about the people in the airplanes? What about their friends and families? Your theory is not holding up in court!" Matthew argued.

"Were you able to talk to any of the victims before they died?" Elizabeth asked.

"No, of course not!" Matthew replied.

"Well, how do you know that they ignored the intervention that was to prevent them from being a victim?" Elizabeth responded.

"Are you going to try to tell me that if everyone had listened to 'something telling them to go home', nobody would have died? Do you realize how ridiculous that sounds?" Matthew asked.

"No. That would be insane; but it would be just as insane to believe that the Spirit did not try to spare some lives, and they ignored the still, small voice that was warning them. Yours was a direct divine intervention. What were the odds of the other case reaching a settlement that morning? Why was yours the next on the docket?" Elizabeth replied. "What about the lives that were spared? Do you see that as being lucky?

Matthew felt the drink in his hand getting warm. The conversation was beginning to become uncomfortable. He is used to having the upper hand in every situation. He was confident that he was out of his jurisdiction on this argument. He had to make a hasty, but polite, escape from this conversation. He responded to Elizabeth's question by offering what he thought would hopefully be his closing remarks. "You know that we could argue both sides of this issue all night, and the case would be declared a mistrial. I can cite the lack of evidence to support this claim. However, you are a most formidable opponent, Miss Elizabeth Angel. I genuinely enjoyed your company and conversation this evening; it has sincerely and truthfully been stimulating and thought provoking! Now, if you will excuse me, I need to get me a fresh drink, and check on Miss Banks. I am sure we will see each other again before the party is over, so I will not say 'good night', but simply say that I hope you enjoy all the festivities this evening"

"Wow! I made the great Matthew Craig avoid a case! I'm sorry! That was totally rude and uncalled for!" Elizabeth apologetically replied. "I very much enjoyed your company and conversation, as well! You are not at all like everyone says you are."

"Yes, I am! You just brought out a different side of me!" Matthew suggested.

"I think that I like this Matthew better," Elizabeth softly responded. "And, by the way, thank you for the compliment. I could tell you were being sincere and not just passing off a worn off pick up line."

Matthew wondered, "Whatever do you mean? Why are you thanking me for enjoying your company?"

Elizabeth shyly looked down and replied, "Earlier in our conversation, you told me that I was beautiful." She lifted

her head and looked directly at Matthew. "That is something a girl never gets tired of hearing, especially when it is
spoken with no ulterior motivation. Good evening to you,
too, Matthew, and tell Miss Banks I'm sorry for detaining
you for so long!"

"Hey, wait a minute! I still do not have your card!"
Matthew reminded her.

Elizabeth insisted, "I already told you! I am not looking
to change jobs anytime in the foreseeable future!"

Matthew persisted, "I know; you have made that crystal
clear this evening! I am merely being selfish! It never hurts
to call you to try to persuade you to change your mind from
time to time! Besides, if we worked together, we could have
more of these wonderful trials we were having earlier!"

Elizabeth boasted, "It wouldn't be fair to you. You could
not handle losing!"

"I never lose," Matthew responded confidently.

"What would you call your case this evening?" Elizabeth
asked.

"I would say that I was granted a continuance in the
case!" Matthew chuckled. "Would it help my case if I said
that I wanted the card personally, I mean, it's nothing to do
with business? Would you consider taking time from your
busy schedule to talk to an over-hyped attorney?"

Elizabeth smiled softly. She reached into her purse,
pulled out a small case, opened it and removed one of her
cards. She looked at it, and then she stretched out her arm
to hand it to Matthew. "Your best bet to reach me would be
to call my cell number. I am in my office on occasion; I just
feel under the circumstances, at least for now, if you wish to
call me it would be best to call me directly. That way, both
of us avoid a plethora of questions!"

"Thank you!" Matthew responded appreciatively. "I
really enjoy talking to you! You realize I could develop a
habit of calling you!" Matthew looked at her card. He smiled;

even her business card seemed to emit a radiant glow. The card was the color of a summer sunrise. The lettering was a beautiful shade of purple that only enhanced the background. "I'll bet you designed your own business card, didn't you?"

"Oh, stop it! That sounded like a line Matthew would use; I mean, the other Matthew would use!" Elizabeth pleaded.

"No, it is the real one, or I think this is the real one," Matthew admitted. "It's the one that you would talk to when he calls!"

"Go on, get out of here! Your date already hates me!" Elizabeth added, "Oh, don't call me on Sunday! It's church day! Unless, of course, it's an emergency, then please call me!"

Matthew smiled, and turned away to get his drink. Everything about Elizabeth was, well, breathtaking. She had an infectious smile. She was a very shapely woman; she was very pleasing on the eyes. And the eyes....ah, yes, those beautiful eyes. They were big, brown, and bright. They seemed to draw you in even more. She was the total package! He shook his head, smiled, and continued on his way to the bar. While waiting for the bartender to prepare his drink, he located Nicole on the dance floor. She seemed to be having a good time without him. He saw this as permission to enjoy his drink before approaching her and offering his apologies for being rude. Just as he finished his drink, the band finished performing the tune they were playing. Matthew thought to himself, "Perfect timing, or just dumb luck, huh?" Then, after realizing his thought, he chuckled aloud.

Three

"So, I was beginning to think that you had abandoned me!" Nicole declared, smiling. "I can't believe all of the people that are here this evening!"

Matthew smiled; with her hand inside his arm, Matthew escorted Nicole to a table that was not as accessible to the lights. The glow from the chandelier and the candle that was on the table were just enough. "Yes, there are quite a few of the old money men here tonight as well," Matthew bemoaned as he helped Nicole with her chair.

"Thank you for inviting me Matthew; I am having a wonderful time! I have met several people in the fashion and photography industries already! I think that tonight will be a turning point in my career! You don't know how much this means to me!" Nicole continued excitedly. "I've even met several businessmen that have access to apartments better than the kitchen/living room and bedroom/bathroom that I live in now! I think that tonight is the night that will change my life forever!"

Matthew smiled and nodded in agreement. "I am glad that tonight has been a success for you! I am glad that none of the members of the actor's guild made the list this year; they were an embarrassment to our celebration last year!

Have you met any of the other noteworthy people besides the people in the fashion industry?"

"Not yet, I figured that I should allow you to introduce me to some of them as you work your magic around the room," Nicole admitted.

Matthew confessed, "I do not really want to associate with any of my esteemed colleagues at the moment. I hope you are not disappointed. I know that you wanted to take advantage of this opportunity to gain as much insight and inroads as you possibly could tonight. If you want, you can go make contacts without me. Maybe later we can hit the dance floor if you would like!"

"I would like that very much, Matthew! Are you sure, you do not mind if I go on my own? I feel like I am abandoning you; and you made this possible by inviting me to accompany you! Nicole admitted hesitantly, not knowing how Matthew would respond.

"You know, you could kiss me for good luck," Matthew boldly informed Nicole.

Nicole smiled warmly; her eyes were sparkling with excitement, or maybe it was just the lights. She leaned across the table, wrapped her hand softly around Matthew's neck and placed her soft lips on his. She was deliberate in delaying when she pulled away. She wanted to make sure he knew how much that she appreciated him, and give him a taste of what was yet to come later tonight. "How lucky do you think I will get after that, Matthew?" Nicole asked.

"I would think that you could get almost anything that you put your mind to achieve," Matthew replied. "Go conquer the crowd, and achieve your goals!"

"I'll see you in a little while! Don't forget you owe me a dance!" Nicole giggled back.

Matthew smiled and finished his drink. He watched her as she confidently and zealously approached the president of West Side Bank. He knew that she would be too busy to worry about what he was doing for the next hour or two. "Where was Elizabeth?" he wondered. He needed to talk to her more. He needed to be with her more. She made him forget who he had become, and reminded him of a time when life was not so, well, cold.

"I hope you are not driving tonight, Matthew, that's the second drink you've had so far!" Elizabeth said from behind Matthew at the bar.

"Oh, so now you are keeping tabs on my drinks are you?" Matthew asked. "Okay, I will not have anymore. I don't need them anyway. I like it, but I don't need it. I guess it's one of those habits you get because 'everyone else is doing it', but since when did I care what everyone else was doing? It's not like my morning coffee. I don't so much like it as I <u>need</u> it! I'm very glad you came by. I really enjoy talking with you. Even though you talk about a subject in which I am very uneasy and very uneducated, you do not try to embarrass or ridicule me." Matthew paused. "This is not easy for me, to open up and pour out and talk about what I'm feeling. I have not been able to feel this comfortable with a woman in a long time. See what you've done to me!"

"What do you mean?" Elizabeth gasped in astonishment.

"Before I came to this party, I just lived my life; I had no commitments, no cares, and no worries. I had physical relationships, but that satisfaction was never fulfilling. I always hoped to have more, but it just never happened."

Elizabeth interrupted, "Are you saying that the most eligible bachelor in New York, Matthew Craig, is tired of being a playboy? He wants to settle down and be an old married man?"

"Hey, I was never a playboy! You make me sound so dirty! Yes, I had a few dates! Okay, quite a few dates, but, I was not-oh God-I was a player; but that was not me, or I mean that was not who I wanted to be. That was not part of the plan; it just sort of happened. I mean, it was me, but I became someone else." Matthew tried to explain himself, but seem to be futile in his efforts. "I really am a nice guy who just happens to be incredibly rich and incredibly sure that all that the women want are the prestige that comes with being known as Mrs. Matthew Craig, the bank account that comes with it, and of course the home and the cars. It is not about me at all. Oh, sure, there will be a sexual relationship to pay a penance for the cost of their good life, but they will have affairs while I am at work, and the scandals will be in the news. The divorce will be time in court away from time in court that I could be doing something actually good for someone!" Matthew stopped to think for a moment, took a drink of water from the glass that was at his table, and swallowed hard. "I said too much, didn't I," Matthew asked.

"Confession is good for the soul," Elizabeth said softly. "As I told you earlier, I like this Matthew much, much better than the one everyone else knows. As you already know, I don't need your money. My apartment is bigger than yours is, my social life is boring compared to yours, I can almost speak as eloquent as you, and I am an excellent listener, so I would say that you could feel totally safe with me."

"That's just it, I do feel totally safe with you, and that is in a way, a little frightening," Matthew admitted.

Elizabeth closed her eyes, shook her head slowly for a moment, allowing the preposterousness of the statement fade, then turned to look at Matthew. "Why would you be frightened? You have already admitted some big secrets about yourself, Mr. Craig! These are things that could be used as evidence against you in this little court of ours!"

"Since you brought it up, Miss Angel, and since you now have my evidence before you, would you like to present your evidence before the court? What is the story behind the man in your life? Who is he, and what is his occupation?" Matthew questioned.

Elizabeth smiled uneasily. "There is no man in my life, counsel. Most of the men I meet do not understand what I do for a living, many of them cannot accept my lifestyle, and still many do not accept my faith walk. I do not want nor am I looking for a casual sexual affair. The thing that is really upsetting is that some of the men in the church are even worse than the men I meet outside of the church! They seem to think it is only one little lapse, and if we get married it doesn't matter, anyway! I do not operate in the world of 'ifs'! The others that respect your vow of purity are no better; they want you to change as well! They want you to become 'Suzy Homemaker' and forget about your dreams and aspirations, I mean, hello! God gave me a purpose just as He gave them a purpose. If I were to give up my purpose, just to get married to become a homemaker and raise a family, even if I was in love and I was operating in love and following all of God's laws, I would still be disobedient to Jesus! He had called me to do this and He has not told me it was time to stop doing this yet. Besides, if He wants me to meet someone and to possibly have a future relationship with that person, He will ensure that the person will not ask me to sacrifice anything that He has called me to do, and I will be able to lift up my partner with the same love and support that he will give me! You see, Matthew, unlike you, I can handle being alone, but I do not want to remain alone! However, I will admit that I did not plan nor did I imagine that I would still not be a mother at twenty-eight, much less still be single!"

Matthew sat and soaked in every word spoken by this beautiful woman sitting next to him. "I can handle being alone, and you are right, I do not wish to remain alone. I just do not have a time frame on when this is to transpire! I will admit, that I used to joke that being single would be a fun life; you know, no commitments, no attachments. But, it would be nice to come home to someone to share the excitement and the frustrations of my day. And I never thought that I would still be single at 30 years old!"

"I think I know what is bothering you, Matthew!" Elizabeth revealed.

"Something is bothering me? What makes you think that?" Matthew asked.

"Come on, Matthew, it's just you and me here. You do not have to be that other man tonight. You said yourself that you felt safe with me."

"Okay. What's bothering me?" Matthew inquired of her.

Elizabeth paused a moment, took a deep breath, and sighed. "You, Matthew Craig, are afraid of intimacy."

Matthew laughed aloud so heartily he looked around to see who had heard him. "I'm afraid of intimacy? Did you forget that you earlier alleged that I was guilty of having a relationship with a different woman every week! So how can I be afraid of intimacy?"

Elizabeth shot back, "Sex is not intimacy! Although, when there is true intimacy, there is love, and the physical relationship usually includes some terrific sex, or so I been told, and I believe in my heart that this is true, as well. Your relationships are, as far as the world sees, purely physical; they are of no substance other than the career advancements that your dates may obtain and the photo ops and the sexual satisfaction you gain. Is there more to it, or is what we see what we get?"

"Hey, I care about all of the girls I have ever been with! It's not like I'm just using them as one night stands!" Matthew quickly pointed out.

"Okay, how many of them have you ever been out with on a second date?" Elizabeth asked.

"I don't know, a few of them," Matthew answered.

"Well, how many is a few, counsel, one, two, ten?" Elizabeth continued.

"Alright, alright," Matthew confessed. "Only two of them!"

"Wow! What would the number of women be if we pushed further into the esteemed counsel's private life that he did not have sex with after their date?" Elizabeth continued with her piercing line of questions.

"That's a little personal, don't you think? I can assure you it's not as many as people think and certainly not as many as I would have preferred," Matthew angrily replied. He was, for the first time this evening, upset with Elizabeth. It was not because of the personal questions, it was because it was opening up parts of his past that he wanted to remain sealed forever.

Elizabeth sensed the tension, and could see his noticeable trepidation. "Matthew, I'm so sorry! I was way out of line! But, can't you see I was only trying to make a point? You may think that your decisions do not affect other people's lives if you are unattached to them, but you are wrong! Just because you will not allow yourself to gain an emotional attachment to your clients in the courtroom does not mean that you have not become a part of their life forever! Think about it for a minute! After a case is settled, win or lose"-

"I never lose," Matthew interrupted.

"Okay, after you win your case, you just move on to the next case. It will be forgotten; but let me assure you that not a day goes by that they are not thankful that Matthew Craig was there to enlighten the judge and jury to their circumstances, and allow them to be where they are today! Your actions have caused you and these people, these families, to have a connection together for eternity! The same thing with all of the beautiful models you have dated. How many of them have advanced their careers because of the contacts they have made by being your date?"

"I guess almost all of them have made some minor contacts, some have made some major contacts. I guess even a couple have seen career changing opportunities develop at these functions," Matthew submitted.

"Do you ever think about your old, I mean, past dates?" Elizabeth asked laughingly at herself and her mistake.

Matthew smiled. He loved to hear her laugh. It made him relax. "There have been a couple that could have been something special, but it just wasn't meant to be. My schedule and long hours, their travel and long hours, and neither of them were willing to sacrifice their career for a long-term relationship, so it never happened. It just wasn't meant to be."

"What about before you moved to New York, was there anyone important in your life?" Elizabeth asked. "I mean, I'm sorry, you don't have to tell me if you don't want"-

Matthew interrupted her softly, "It's okay. I don't care to talk about it. There was nobody else in my life. Yes, I had my share of girlfriends, but nothing was ever serious. I wanted to be an attorney, and I knew that a little fun now could cost me a lot later, so I guess I was really just more of a loner. My Mom and Dad were great parents growing up. They were very supportive. They raised us right. They taught us values; certainly something you don't see too much of anymore! I have a sister, too. They were the only important people in my life before New York. I don't see too much of my family since I moved here in the city. My sister still lives back home. She's going to college and helps take care of Mom and Dad when she is not at school or at the hospital and when she's on break. She wants to be the world's best surgeon. She's much smarter than I am! She's majoring in neurology with a minor in oncology. I wish I had her energy, her enthusiasm! I am so proud of her!"

"What is your sister's name?" Elizabeth asked.

"It's Mandy. Her name was from an old Barry Manilow song back in the 1970's! Can you believe it?" Matthew asked laughingly.

Elizabeth is now laughing almost uncontrollably. "You do know that the Mandy that Barry Manilow was writing and singing about was a dog?"

"My sister is a very beautiful young woman!" Matthew quickly replied, before he could no longer contain himself laughing, "Who just happens to be named after a dog!" He was amazed at the maturity and the intelligence of his baby sister. She was just now twenty-three years old; he knew he was not even in her league when he was that age. But then again, he never has been in her league. She graduated high school before her sixteenth birthday; He thought about her excitement when he gave her a car for her birthday to allow her to travel to and from school in a dependable vehicle, without the worry of mechanical problems. In case something should happen, she also had the satellite service in her car with the GPS monitoring to locate her if she should ever need it. Now she was determined to finish her medical schooling before she turns twenty-five, or so it seems. One thing is certain: Matthew loves to talk about his sister. He is very proud of her and her accomplishments.

"How is Mandy able to manage all of it, I mean, medical school is quite expensive! Does she have a scholarship, grants, and I hope student loans are able to help?" a very concerned Elizabeth asked. "Where is she attending college? Is she also attending Duke, like her big brother?"

"Yes, thankfully, she does have a partial scholarship, and she was able to secure two small grants, however, whatever else she needs she just needs to call her big brother. And yes, she is attending her old brother's alma mater, Duke University. I do not want her to have to struggle or worry about anything the way that I did. It's not that I had anything to worry about except for staying out of trouble at the student union parties at the end of each year. I think that my struggles back then, whether real or imagined, made me a better attorney today." Matthew confided.

"Well, I'd say you are making up for lost time now, huh, Matthew," Elizabeth questioned.

"Hey, you know what, enough with the Romeo, the gigolo, playboy, or whatever else you want to call me. The joke is dead as of now." Matthew seemed genuinely hurt. "I can count on my hands the number of women that have gone back to my apartment, and the number that I have actually had sex with is even less! So there you have it! I just put holes in that theory of my wild lifestyle image! How do you respond now, counsel?"

Elizabeth had to stop the smile that was forming on her face. "All I can say is the prosecution rests."

Matthew smiled. "Very well said! Very well said! And thankfully, it is about time!"

About the time Matthew was about to ask Elizabeth to dance, Nicole come running to the table as fast as she could, considering the dress and the shoes that she was wearing. "Matthew, I'm so sorry to interrupt you from your meeting"-

Matthew interrupted, "It's okay. It's not a meeting. We were just having a very absorbing conversation! Nicole Banks, I would like to introduce you to Elizabeth Angel! Elizabeth Angel, this is Nicole Banks!"

"It's an honor to meet you Nicole Banks," Elizabeth said as she held out her hand.

Nicole gushed as she shook her hand, "Wow, it's a pleasure to meet you, Elizabeth Angel! That's really awesome, don't you think, Matthew? Her name is Angel, and she looks just like an angel!" Nicole giggled, and continued her conversation at her rapid pace. "Oh, I need to speak with you privately for a moment, if I may. Could I possibly take him away from you for a moment, Miss Angel?"

"Certainly, take him as long as you need. He is your date, remember?" Elizabeth replied.

Nicole laughed, "He is, isn't he? I promise I will not take long. It was very nice meeting you Miss Angel!"

Matthew thought about what Nicole had said. She does look like an angel! Is that why it is so easy to talk to her? He had other things to deal with at the moment besides satisfying his curiosity. "Nicole, what is wrong?"

Nicole was so excited she was shivering. "Nothing, well, I hope nothing! You see, while I have been out mingling, I met Trevor Allen! Do you Know who that is? He's like the biggest fashion and personal photographer in the world right now! Every model appearing in anything from People to Playboy wants Trevor taking their pictures! Well, he has asked me if he could be my personal photographer as long as I was not under contract with anyone else at this time!"

Matthew looked puzzled. "Well, that's like a good thing, am I correct?"

Nicole replied, "Yes, that's a very good thing! But here is the thing; you see, he has already left the party because he has a photo shoot at his studio at 10:30. He asked if I could be at his studio at 11:30 to discuss a possible deal. I was really looking forward to tonight, and I know that you probably had plans tonight as well, but"-

Matthew grabbed Nicole, wrapped his arms around her and gently kissed her soft and very inviting lips. He could feel the firmness of her breast as he held her to his chest. Her heart was racing; he hoped that he was the cause of her excitement, but he wasn't convinced. But at this very moment, it didn't matter. The dress she was wearing allowed him to experience the tenderness of her skin as his hands gently caressed her soft, warm, and very inviting back. His fingers acted as if he was a blind man and they were reading the pages of a very enthralling novel. He kissed her again, with more force behind this one, but still not hard, then kissed her neck, and finally on the cheek. "No buts. I understand. Maybe we can get together again if you don't run off and become Miss Supermodel or something. Good luck with uh, Trevor. Good night, Nicole." His body was telling him that he would regret letting her leave, but his mind, as well as his heart, was elsewhere.

Elizabeth was not listening to the conversation, but she was watching with great intensity.... and great interest.

Four

Everything so far tonight has been happening at an exhausting pace. As he watched Nicole walk away, he thought about how the evening had gone up until now. The conversations have gone everywhere from religion to work to...home. Matthew had not thought much about New Hope, North Carolina, since he left ten years ago. New Hope, located in Franklin County in the eastern part of North Carolina, is as small town as you can get. The *county* has a population of about 50,000 people, and it is home to the oldest junior college in the United States, which is Louisburg College, founded in 1787. Louisburg is also the county seat.

The main industries there now are wood products, plastic recycling, and software development, and the economy based mostly on agriculture, lumber, and textiles. Agriculture helped support his family for several years before his father became a member of the management staff of the recycling plant. Many of the old things are gone now. He remembers how much his Dad hated it when the railroad stopped running. If it weren't for the resiliency and the strong ethic, moral, and religious beliefs of the people, New Hope would not have ever survived.

It is only about an hour drive from three world-class universities: Duke University in Durham, the University of North Carolina at Chapel Hill, and North Carolina State University. He eventually chose Duke University, mainly due to the outstanding law degree programs at the college, as well as the many other conveniences that the large city of Durham can offer. Duke University allowed him to get a superior law degree and still enjoy the quietness of country living; the escapism that he felt was essential to obtaining a law degree with the level of knowledge he wanted to acquire. The peace and tranquility of living at home in a small town while going to college, and New Hope was small town America. As far as Matthew was concerned, if you listened to John Mellencamp's 'Small Town', it is about New Hope.

Now Mandy is in her eighth year at Duke, working at the hospital and working on yet another degree, experiencing the same benefits of New Hope and home that he did, and she is flourishing! She is also working at the University Hospital, and is beginning to build a strong relationship with several patients. She is going to be known everywhere in the country, maybe the world, as a great surgeon, and it will be someday soon. She has great compassion for people, she is very patient with them; she has an uncanny ability to seemingly know what they are trying to say even though the words they are saying do not convey it.

It was always easy for him to talk to Mandy. He loved being the big brother when they were growing up, and still loves being the big brother, although the conversations have changed considerably. It seems as if she helps him more than he can help her now. He misses the days when she was knocking on his bedroom door to ask him questions, like, "Why did God make the night sky so beautiful with all the stars and the purple shadows dusting the sky if everybody is going to be asleep and can't see it?" Her wisdom was a nuisance at times, but it was painfully obvious she was destined for bigger and better things.

She has always had an inner peace and an aura of confidence about her. It was something that you noticed immediately when you met her. She was full of life; she was full of love. She was radiant; her tan is not the thing that made her astonishing, it was her presence. But it is not her physical presence, either, even though she is a very beautiful young woman, for a sister, which poses another worry for Matthew. Many men are out there that are like him; there are even more that are worse than he is. It's just something about her that says 'I'm special'. The same aura he had seen when he walked into the party this evening. The same aura he sees around Elizabeth.

As Matthew turned around to rejoin the party, he realized that he was the focus of Elizabeth's attention. He felt guilty for leaving her alone, but instantaneously felt a twinge of accomplishment as her eyes told him that she was longing for more conversation. Actually, he was hoping for more of her conversation, as well. He remembers that the conversation was quite disconcerted when Nicole so timely interrupted it earlier. Will it begin where it ended? That will be up to Elizabeth. One thing was certain: Matthew did not care to talk about family, just do not make him talk about himself. He hopes to shift the focus of the conversation to Elizabeth. He wants to know more about her; much more.

Elizabeth instinctively knew that she was going to be the topic of conversation when Matthew returned to the table. She was ready. She had been on a wonderful journey in her mind while he was away with Nicole, reminiscing about her days growing up in beautiful, sunny Miami, Florida. She, unlike Matthew, was an only child; she had been, on more than one occasion, called a "spoiled brat". Her parents were very protective and somewhat strict, but as she got older, they allowed her the freedom to go out to learn about things and make decisions on her own. She definitely lived in the right place to enjoy an abundance of culture. Almost every ethnic group you can name lived in or near Miami. There were several museums in or near Miami, which were a fascination as a child. To help her with what she may not have learned from the museums, she enjoyed talking with elderly men and women she met at the nursing home she volunteered at after school. She enjoyed the white sandy beaches, all the water, and there were plenty of malls for her and her friends to shop and hang out. Life was fun, but in her senior year of high school, Elizabeth realized she wanted more from life than just "all this". Many people would consider this paradise, and that is wherein she had her biggest problem. She had seen all of the things that Miami had to offer; she knows there is a dark and ugly side that many do not see. 'Miami Vice' and 'CSI: Miami' brought and continue to bring attention to a beautiful city, but that is a two-edged sword. She had also learned over the years from talking to the ones that have migrated here from Cuba, Uganda, Africa, and Mexico. There were many others, but these were the ones that left an image painted so vividly in her mind that she could not imagine the tragedy and horrific events that are going on daily in those countries. When she told her parents of her plans to attend college and with aspirations of a double major in humanities and theology, they were very excited. Suddenly, her Dad's countenance had become very reserved. She could not recall ever seeing him this way.

"Liz, this is a huge undertaking you are about to endure. You cannot possibly succeed if you stay in Miami. Have you given thought about where you would like to go to school?" her Dad asked with apprehension. "Where will you go to college?"

Elizabeth was still hearing her Dad's question in her mind and did not hear Matthew talking to her when he sat down.

"Where did you go to college?" Matthew asked. "Hello! Elizabeth! Elizabeth! Are you all right?"

"Uh-oh, yes, I'm sorry, Matthew! I was thinking about something and got lost in the moment. Did you say something?" Elizabeth asked in a nonchalant manner.

"I was trying to ask you where you went to college. You know I'm a Blue Devil from Duke University; I was just wondering who I was up against tonight."

"Oh, I went to Seton Hall in New Jersey; go Pirates!" Elizabeth cheered.

"You know, to some we would be considered enemies. Especially if you talk to the die-hard basketball fans, or should I say fanatics at Duke!" Matthew informed. "So, did this Jersey girl just cross over to New York to move up or to move out?"

"Actually," Elizabeth paused, "I look at it as my current stop on the journey. It started in Miami, and then it went to New Jersey, then a summer in Zimbabwe, back to New Jersey, another summer abroad in Uganda and Ethiopia, then back to New Jersey. Now during all of this were many weekend and Christmas break flights back to Miami. Finally, I end up here in Manhattan. I have enough frequent flyer miles to take my next two trips wherever I want to go for free!"

"Wow! My favorite sports teams are in Miami! Man, I would have loved that! Who am I kidding? I would love it now! I'll bet it would be great in October if the Marlins would be in the World Series! You could watch a baseball game, catch the Heat in a basketball game possibly the next night, and on Sunday, watch the Dolphins in a football game! Oh man, that would be a perfect week! "Are you a sports fan? What is your favorite sport? What is your favorite team?

Elizabeth groaned. "You are even worse than most of the fans that actually live there! Why are you a fan of my hometown teams?"

"Well, the first football game that I remember watching was the Super Bowl when Miami was playing San Francisco. I guess I chose Miami because of the quarterback, Dan Marino"-

"He was a great one," Elizabeth interrupted.

"Yes, he was, and I also liked the uniforms!" Matthew continued. "When you are a kid it is okay to choose based on color recognition or your favorite colors. Anyway, the Marlins were a new team and I wanted to stay with a team that I thought would become a winner, which it did; as I always say, I never lose! Finally, their basketball team, well, that is another story. I really don't have an explanation other than I just chose them. Maybe subconsciously I was staying in one city, I don't know. But it has worked out really well! 'Zo is one of my favorite players of all time."

"Zo?" Elizabeth asked. "Do you know all of the players on a nickname basis?"

Matthew continued, "Alonzo Mourning! Come on, you know"-

"Yes, I know! I just couldn't resist!" Elizabeth explained through her laughter.

I'm sorry, Elizabeth! I tend to be a bit zealous when it comes to sports! That is my escape from the world! Now, please tell me, how much fun was it growing up in Miami? The beach, the sun, and endless fun; there's something to do all through the year, huh?" Matthew asked enthusiastically.

Elizabeth nodded in disagreement. "I guess when you live there you don't see it that way. Oh, don't get me wrong, I loved living in Miami! There were, and are, lots of things about the city that make it great! You mentioned some of them- but there is also the art and historical museums, our zoos, of course our sports teams, and our many other family attractions are part of what make the city great. I loved the diversity of the cultures; you could appreciate it, Matthew, being an attorney! Persecuted in their country before coming to America, most of them for their religious beliefs, they were willing to pay whatever price they had to bring themselves and their families to our country, even if it cost them their life!" Elizabeth's eyes began welling up with tears. "The stories of injustice would infuriate you, Matthew! I know, because they break my heart! This is just one chapter of the sad saga of our fair city. The other is the glamorization of an immoral lifestyle that is evident and prevalent along the strip, downtown, and Miami Beach. The nightclubs, the bars, and other businesses that are seedy at best are too numerous to count. Sex and drugs are commonplace; and wherever the two are, violence and death seem to follow. It is an issue I hope to tackle someday when I am finished with my current mission."

Matthew sighed, "Those activities are everywhere. What do you think is going on here tonight, I mean, for the most part, anyway?"

Elizabeth quickly responded, "I understand that! Yes, it is everywhere, but it is the way that Miami, in movies or on television, is fallaciously portrayed by glamorizing the lifestyle, and making the danger seem like a rush! The criminals use real bullets, and you end up really dead! I have seen too many people die senseless deaths just because they wanted to 'be cool' and be a part of 'the scene'. I've even lost several friends, some were classmates. I know it's a different time and a different era. Matthew, trust me on this! I lived there for eighteen years; the scenery changes, the people changes, the poisons of choice changes, but the game is the same."

Matthew was impressed with her ability to deliver a presentation politically. "What about the police and the drug task forces? Are they not acting upon this to clean up these areas?" Matthew continued. "Why has it not improved in all this time, if it was bad when you were a child? I remember when the country focused its attention back in the mid-1980s every Friday night when 'Miami Vice' came on television.

The cops that were in the television series were always under scrutiny and suspicion. They were also a rather rough looking team, if you ask me. I know the drug task force has to have 'the look', but let me ask about the officers that assist. Do they really feel it is worth their salary to risk their life to stop a losing battle? Am I correct to assume that it is a losing battle? I mean, if it was as prevalent then as it is today, why can't any progress be made?"

"I think that Miami/Dade County has one of the best forces in the country! It is simple mathematics, really! There is too much drugs, too much crime, far too many homicides to investigate, and not enough budget to do more! I think they get more out of their dollars than any other department, well, maybe New York, they do a great job, too, than any other department in the United States! You've got to remember that the drug dealers have unlimited amounts of money. They are not just selling in Miami; they are in Detroit, Chicago, and not just the big cities, but also the smaller ones like Huntington, West Virginia and in Columbus, Ohio. They have more people than our forces have. The one thing they do not have is heart! Our force has a heart and the desire to see a safe and drug free city for their families. That is what drives them; that is their motivation! The dealer and his pushers only thought is money and survival. If we are going to win this war, and I believe we will, it is going to be because the people will see that desire and will help them to track down and eradicate the leeches that are draining the life from our city!"

"So, do you miss home, Elizabeth?" Matthew asked hesitantly.

Five

Elizabeth paused, and then smiled the smile that lit up the room. "I have been going on a bit, haven't I? That is the privilege of being an only child. I'm allowed to talk as much as I want! Can I please finish my thought? So far, I have painted a very poor picture of my hometown. But the fact is, it is a very good city! It has some of the best schools in the country. It has some of the best doctors and hospitals, as well. Our university is among the best in the world. We are on the cutting edge of experiments and discoveries. We are among the leaders in breakthroughs in medical science, aerospace engineering, and digital technology. We have some of the best restaurants in the world; we have some of the best chefs, as well. We have many different places to enjoy a vacation. We have a beautiful beach. We have great museums. However, most importantly, we have several churches for all of our many ethnic groups to hear the Word of God, and learn how to enrich their lives and live a joyous life. Okay, I'm through now! We were talking about you before. Tell me more about you and Mandy! Where was home for you growing up?"

"We grew up in a little town, actually it is not considered populated enough to be considered a town I guess, but it is called New Hope, North Carolina. It was a place where you could go out and get lost in your thoughts and the only thing that would interrupt you would be the whistle of the New Hope Valley Railroad as it was passing through! It was peace, quiet, and lots of fun! We had plenty of mischief we could create in and around all the farms and ranches. I had a lot of wonderful quiet times when I would just walk along the railroad tracks. Mandy says it is still just as peaceful at home, and the boys are still just as mischievous! It's as you said; some things never change! I had a fun, even if it was an uneventful childhood when compared to yours. I had lightning bugs for nightlights. Mandy has enjoyed pretty much the same things.

Our Dad's name is Jacob, and our mother's name is Natalie. Our Dad went from farming to recycling, and our Mom was a, well, Mom! She was home whenever we needed her. She was a superior cook, we never worried or fussed about going out to eat; however, whenever Dad would receive a bonus at work, he was quick to give Mom a day off! He would get up early the next morning; well, he would wake me up, too in order to get the chores done before Mom would wake up. Mandy always wanted to help, but Dad wouldn't let her. He always told her we needed someone to keep Mom occupied if she woke up! Mom didn't get many chances to sleep in; whenever the opportunity arose she welcomed the blessing eagerly! After Dad and I finished, we would come back inside to take a shower before we would make breakfast for everyone. After everyone was finished, Mom and Dad always went for a walk, and Mandy and I would do the dishes. Whenever they returned from their walk, we would all sit down and name places we would like to go when we went to town. Twice a year, bonus or no bonus, Mom and Dad went to town by themselves. Dad always loved doing everything as a family, but he always said that two days were just for Mom! On those days, we would usually stay home and watch movies, and once Mandy was older, we would visit our neighbors and offer to help them with any tasks around the house that they may not be able to do anymore. We used to make stupid little jokes about their "dates", but we realized the importance and the significance of those times. I mean, I will never forget how much Dad spoiled Mom. I sometimes think he enjoyed their dates more than Mom did! Mom and Dad more than just love each other; they respect each other, they like spending all of their free time together and with us kids! We need a lot more love like that in the world!

I never told you about our neighbors, Miss Bessey and Mr. Bolden! We enjoyed our visits with them; they always had such great stories to tell. The history lessons we received through them were more vivid, picturesque, and much more informative than any taught in school! Mr. Bolden served in two wars and he has several medals and scars to prove it. Miss Bessey was a nurse for forty-two years! She still visits the nursing home and talks with many of the patients; many of them are younger than she is! I would think that they are both in their mid-eighties now, if not older. Mandy has not said anything of their passing, so I assume they are still doing well. Everyone helped everyone, really. If one person was hurting, everyone pitched in to help. Our preacher would let us know about it on Sunday or Wednesday if more needed to be done. Everyone worked hard, and we played just as hard, too. Looking at the marriages in our tightly woven little community, I'd say that they loved just as hard, as well. Most of the people that I knew as I grew up in New Hope are still married. I mean, here in New York, marriages that last 48 weeks get as much fanfare as the 48 year marriages back home in New Hope."

Elizabeth gazed at Matthew with the softest and most gentle stare he had ever experienced. "You know, Matthew, it is no coincidence that you and Mandy were born and raised in a town called 'New Hope' as that is precisely what the two of you do with your lives daily. You offer people new hope. Mandy does it with her kind words, and her ability to understand her patient's fears and put them at ease. She makes them believe that they will be well again. You do it by giving your clients hope that they have an opportunity to get their home, their finances, their dignity, even their life back. That is giving people hope. Do you have any idea how blessed you are?"

Matthew tried to shrug it off. "They pay handsomely for all of the hours that I work on their case. I have sacrificed many things in my life to be able to do what I do."

"Are you complaining, Matthew? Because, no one forced you to make the choices you have made! You became the attorney that you are today because you are dedicated, driven, and focused. That is just who you are. You have a heart for helping people, whether you choose to admit it or not. And when you put those personality traits together, we have you! God made you this way, because there is no one else that can do what you do!" Elizabeth explained.

Matthew had to laugh. "Okay Reverend Elizabeth! Tell me this, why do I continue to enslave myself with work? I could leave New York tomorrow, move to any small town in America, relax for at least two years, and then start up a private practice! Hey, I could even sell two of my cars and take another year off! Why do I subject myself to this? I can still help others somewhere else, could I not?"

Elizabeth wasted no time with her response. "Yes, of course, you can! But you are here in New York for a purpose! Would you have amassed your great fortune if you were in a small town? Would you have four cars in your small town practice? Would you be as renowned in your small town as you are in New York? You know that you would not be able to undertake the vast diversity of cases in your small town that you are able to experience here in New York! Besides, you would not have been able to have a date with Nicole or any of the other beauties you have met while here in New York if you were in your small town practice! And last and probably most important, you would not have been able to have such an intriguing argument with me if you were not here in New York!"

Matthew was unprepared for the comments that Elizabeth just made, especially the last one. Everything that she had said was true, but he had not become an attorney to get rich. Of course, he knew that he could have a very comfortable lifestyle with the financial rewards that come with being a successful attorney. He enjoyed the drama, the excitement, and the challenges that each new day presented in a courtroom. He also knew, while still in college, that to be successful, you had to be among the elite in order to be recognized. That is what he purposed in his mind and in his heart to do; he was going to pour all of his energy into his education and thus allow him to become one of the best legal minds in our country. But what had he given up? Time. He sacrificed time with family, time with friends, and time to develop any relationship in his life to share his dreams and goals in order to obtain the brass ring. Although he still talked frequently with Mandy, very few people that knew anything about what was happening in his life. In addition, after the events of 9/11, when he further purposed that he would not allow himself to develop any feelings in his heart for anyone, in order to avoid the pain of loss that he experienced during those dark days that followed, he had become obsessed with work. The reality of it now is that he has become so successful, that he does not have time to invest into developing a relationship. Tonight, he is not regretting it as much as he did before he met this most stunning and intriguing woman that was sitting with him. Maybe there really was a purpose to his career path detouring through New York City after all.

"I must concur with all of your statements, counsel. But you did not explain how God has allowed me to get to this point in my life."

"Okay, now think back. Whose idea was it for you to become an attorney?" Elizabeth asked. "Did your parents encourage you or was it your choice?"

"It was mine. I always loved a good debate in school, and I loved trying to solve the cases on the television shows before they would reveal the verdict. There were several shows that the writers made mistakes and I would catch them. It drove Dad nuts! I just thought that since this was something that I really liked, and it seemed like a very good job to be able to be financially well off, so it seemed like the logical choice. I loved sports, but I know I was not good enough to pursue it as a professional career."

"So, do you see? This is your purpose in your life! God has given you a gift! You enjoy your job; it has allowed you to maintain a very comfortable lifestyle and you get to help those in need while doing it!" Elizabeth explained. "Did you just say, 'I am going to be a lawyer someday', or did something inside of you tell you that this is what you were meant to do?"

"I guess it was an intuition inside of me. I remember a feeling, it was as if it was telling me, 'this is your destiny; you are good at this, so, go for it!' I really do not know how else to explain it."

Elizabeth continued, "That was the Spirit prompting you to your purpose! See, I told you that God talks to you; all you need to do is listen! He knows what is best for you! And me as well!"

Matthew asked puzzlingly, "So I owe it all to God, right? Is that what you are telling me? I know that He is in control of everything, or He can control everything; so please explain to me why He allowed the attack on the Twin Towers? Why did all of those people have to die? And not just them, what about flight 93, and the attack on the Pentagon? What about their purpose?"

Elizabeth could see the pain and the passion that Matthew had for these people still bottled inside of him. She thought for a moment before she answered his question, and silently asked God for direction in her answers to help him understand. "I'm sorry that you lost many of your friends, Matthew. It really was their time to die. It was a senseless act of hate against our country, and against our religion. The people that attacked us hate Christianity, as their twisted view of the Muslim theology believes they are to kill everyone that does not follow their beliefs. You have to remember that we live in a world that is full of sin, and that the devil is lord of the earth. We allow Jesus Christ to be Lord of our lives when we accept Him as Savior, and therefore we are no longer citizens of the U.S., but citizens of the Kingdom of Heaven! Even though we live here, we are foreigners, you might say. Yes, God could have stopped the planes, but that would be interfering in satan's realm. Jesus cannot come to this realm unless He is invited; He is always watching over us and always listening to us. Unless we cry out to Jesus for His intervention and His wisdom, the events of earth are played out according to man's will!"

Matthew shrugged his shoulders then protested, "What about the Christians that were killed? What about the purpose God had for them?"

Six

"Do you really think that they would wish to come back to this chaotic world and leave Paradise? I would be willing to bet that they were comforted during their moment of fear. Yes, sometimes Christians are a victim of an assault of fear. It all depends upon their strength in the Lord that determines if they choose to remain in fear. Do you remember hearing about the apartment fire in West Virginia not long ago? The three siblings that died together in that fire were afraid, but as they were talking to their mother on a cell phone, she also heard them singing songs of Praise to Jesus. They wanted to get out alive, but they also knew that if they did not, they had a promise of eternal life with Jesus, and that was their comfort. It was what allowed them to praise Him in the midst of their storm. When was the last time you prayed, Matthew," Elizabeth asked.

"I really can't remember. It must have been back when all of the events in September 2001, were going on. I mean, it was a very frantic and very hectic time," Matthew recalled.

"Do you think that the court proceedings of September 11th were just a mere coincidence? Did you not tell me that you had an appointment cancelled with a client in one of the Towers to allow you to appear in court that morning?

Somebody was praying for you, Matthew! I would be willing to bet if you were to be honest or remember the events that followed, someone that has a close relationship with the Lord revealed to you that they had prayed for you that morning, or even the night before!"

Matthew felt all the color drain from his face. His mind immediately went back in time to September of 2001. He could see it as vividly as the time it occurred. Mandy had called him the night before. She had told him that she felt uneasiness in her spirit. She had told him to be careful tomorrow, and that she was praying for me. She said that she knew that everything would turn out just as Christ Jesus has planned, but she still needed to call to tell me, and to say, 'I love you!' She ended the phone call by telling me that she would not have to worry about her big brother if he would just turn his life over to God. Now Mandy has enlisted reinforcements; she has someone from her army of believers here in New York to work on big brother now! "Elizabeth, I know that whatever it is gives you and Mandy this....this peace, a confidence about you, an obvious presence about you that draws people to you.....but, I need evidence that this God that I grew up learning about is as real today as He was then! The way things have been in the world the last few years has me in serious doubt!" Matthew pleaded.

Elizabeth pleaded, "It is more like you have serious denial! You want obvious, but you are living oblivious! The Lord inundates with evidence several times a day and yet you remain unaware of all the gifts and the miracles that are taking place around you constantly and consistently in your life! Forgive me Matthew, but I need to ask you! Did you ever accept Jesus as your Savior when you were in North Carolina? Have you done it since you moved to New York?"

Matthew was uncomfortable with the question. "Being a Christian did not protect any of them from the terrorist attacks on 9/11! What about all of the people that are killed in the senseless suicide bombings? I guess I have been an attorney too long; I need to know more before I will be convinced!"

Elizabeth sighed, "It is all based on faith! You must accept on faith, and stand firm on your belief as this allows your faith to grow! It is *all* about faith! You have to trust, and accept what you cannot see to settle this one! This is one where visible, tangible evidence will not be available. If you face the Lord without having accepted Jesus as your personal Savior, you are doomed! Being an attorney will be of no use to you then! He will be the judge and jury, and your verdict cannot change! It was determined before you die; you determine your verdict here on earth!"

Matthew looked at his watch. It was already 11:50 PM, and it seems like only moments, not hours ago that he arrived. However, now the time was moving slowly. He was feeling the heaviness of his situation. He could also see that Elizabeth was waiting for a response. "I'm sorry, Elizabeth! I just cannot reach back in time and bring back everything that I heard in church years ago! I have been calloused by the many tragedies that have occurred in our world since I moved to New York in August of 1998. I want to believe that God does still care, and that He is real, but it is going to take Him revealing Himself to me to make me believe! Please pray for me!" Matthew could not believe the words that had just come out of his mouth. He cannot recall if he had *ever* asked anyone to pray for him before in his life!

Elizabeth, being in harmony with her Savior, could recognize the mesmerized expression on Matthew's face. She was ready. "Matthew, the fact that you asked me to pray for you should tell you that somewhere inside of that hard, protective wall you have erected is a believer. I will tell you this- if you want the Lord to reveal Himself to you, He will! All you have to do is ask, and be receptive to hear His words!"

They were both too busy in conversation all evening to realize that the host of the festivities tonight recognized both of them for their many various accomplishments this past year. None of that mattered to either of them at this moment. They were, just as they have nearly the entire evening, enjoying the company of one another. Elizabeth looked at her watch, and with an astonished look on her face, turned to stare directly into Matthew's eyes. "I'm sorry, but it is getting late; I really have to go! This evening has been one of the best evenings I can remember having since I moved here! Thank you, Matthew for making tonight such a memorable evening!"

Matthew and Elizabeth stood up simultaneously. Matthew grasped her hand and embraced it for what seemed like moments before he spoke. "This *has* been the best night I have experienced since I moved here," Matthew softly announced. "I wish you would reconsider. Please stay longer!"

"I can't; tomorrow is Sunday, and I will need to get at least a little sleep before church tomorrow, oops, later this morning! It is rude to fall asleep in church, you know! I will probably be yawning as it is now!"

Elizabeth's words were shaky. She did not want to leave; she was enjoying the company of a man for the first time in years. There was no tension, and Matthew did not seem to be applying any pressure on her for anything other than conversation. However, her commitment was to her faith, her God; and that means she will sacrifice her own pleasure and enjoyment tonight to allow her to be faithful to Him with her attendance in church services on Sunday. The thoughts that were racing through her head....and her heart were tearing her apart. "Surely He would understand if I was not there this one Sunday! He knows how long I have waited to have a conversation with a respectable man, and the respect be reciprocated with me as well! Wait a minute! I can't do that! There are people that expect to see me this morning! I have commitments to fulfill at church! I have to be there for that! Is it pertinent that I am there, or is it just me thinking that it is? Am I making it about myself or about You? Oh, God help me!"

While allowing those thoughts to clutter her mind, she realized Matthew was still clutching onto her hand. It was a firm, yet soft clutch. His hands were very warm, and very inviting. It felt as if her hands fit perfectly into his. Her mind was beginning to wander again when Matthew broke the silence.

"Are you sure you cannot stay? At least let me drive you home!" Matthew insisted.

"Thanks, but I have a car that is waiting. I usually leave these things by 11:00 PM, but on the odd chance I did stay tonight, I told the driver to arrive at midnight. As you can see, I am *very* late! I hope that my boss is not angry on Monday!" Then her voice became softer, quieter; she was leaving herself vulnerable, even if for just a moment. "I really enjoyed spending time with you, Matthew! I wish that I had a chance to know you better, but I do know that the man I met tonight is not the man society makes him out to be! And I promise I will pray for you when I get home. I know that He will answer my prayer...and he will answer yours, too."

Matthew continued to cradle her hand. Then he pulled her closer to him, lifted her hand to his lips, and softly kissed the back of her hand. Gazing into her soft eyes, Matthew asked, "Would it be alright if I hugged you goodnight?"

Elizabeth smiled warmly, and her eyes seemingly acquired a sparkle. Without an answer, she wrapped her arms around Matthew. Immediately, his arms were around Elizabeth as well. She was soft, warm, and so easy to hold. She felt *good* in his arms. She felt as she *belonged* there. Matthew softly whispered in her ear, "Thank you for tonight.

I will remember this as long as I live. Please say you will see me again!"

Elizabeth enjoyed the embrace as well. She did not feel obligated to be there. She was never worried about any further expectations from Matthew, as his reputation was wrongly tainted. His arms, his embrace, it was like his hand holding; soft, warm...but this was *so* much nicer. "I would like that very much, Matthew! Just call the organization when you have free time!"

Elizabeth was enjoying this moment to its end, but she knew that she had to leave. She pulled back her arms kissed Matthew on his cheek, and pulled away to leave. "I will be waiting to hear from you! Good night, Matthew!"

Matthew could still feel the warmth and the gentleness of her kiss long after she had walked away. His eyes continued to follow her as she got into her waiting car, and then drive away. Now, being alone, he sensed no reason to continue to permeate the premises. He quickly excused himself, shaking hands with several well-wishers and receiving several congratulatory pats on the back He sat down in his car, stared aimlessly into the sky, and then closed his eyes for a moment. After taking a deep breath, Matthew exhaled sharply, and then he sighed, "Lord, if what Elizabeth said is true, that you do still care, and I have a purpose in all of this madness, please reveal proof to me!" One thing Matthew will remember soon is 'Be careful what you wish for!'

Elizabeth arrived home tired, but not as she was from previous engagements in recent memory. She had experienced a wonderful evening, met a very interesting, handsome, and troubled young man in Matthew Craig. She was glad that she got the opportunity to meet him. She was able to determine that he is not the man that everyone says that he is. They only base their assumptions on what they see in his life on a daily basis. They only see snippets of his life; they are not with him for an extended time to verify their assessment. She only spent a few hours with him but she felt as if she knew more about him than anyone else in New York.

After getting ready for bed, Elizabeth retired to her bedroom to read her Bible as she does every night before she goes to sleep. She had a reading plan that she usually follows nightly, but tonight it had changed. She felt a stirring in her spirit to read something else. She felt led to several different places at once, but it all seemed so organized. First, she turned to John 16:13. Jesus was saying, "Howbeit when he, the Spirit of truth, is come, he will guide you into all truth: for he shall not speak of himself; but whatsoever he shall hear, *that* shall he speak: and he will show you things to come." Then, she turned to Acts 17:27, which reads, "That they should seek the Lord, if haply they might feel after him, and find him, though he be not far from every one of us:"

The passages continued to flow; she had to write them down they were flowing to her so rapidly. II Corinthians 4:3-4, James 1:5-8, Hebrews 11:6, Galatians 6:3-8, 1John 1:9, Proverbs 16:9, and the last one was Acts 2:17. She went back to begin reading the ones she had just written down. II Corinthians 4:3-4 reads, "But if the gospel be hid, it is hid to them that are lost: In whom the god of this world hath blinded the minds of them that believe not, lest the light of the glorious gospel of Christ, who is the image of God, should shine unto them." James 1:5-8 reads, "If any of you lack wisdom, let him ask of God, that giveth to all men liberally, and upbraideth not; and it shall be given to him. But let him ask in faith, nothing wavering. For he that wavereth is like a wave of the sea driven with the wind and tossed. For let not a man think that he shall receive any thing of the Lord. A double minded man is unstable in all his ways." Hebrews 11:6 reads, "But without faith it is impossible to please him: for he that cometh to God must believe that he is, and that he is a rewarder of them that diligently seek him."

Elizabeth was feeling a bit overwhelmed; however, she continued reading. Galatians 6:3-8 reads, "For if a man thinketh himself to be something, when he is nothing, he deceiveth himself. But let every man prove his own work, and then shall he have rejoicing in himself alone, and not in another. For every man shall bear his own burden. Let him that is taught in the word communicate unto him that teacheth in all good things. Be not deceived; God is not mocked: for whatsoever a man soweth, that shall he also reap. For he that soweth to his flesh shall of the flesh reap corruption; but he that soweth to the Spirit shall of the Spirit reap life everlasting." I John 1:9 reads, "If we confess our sins, he is faithful and just to forgive us our sins, and to cleanse us from all unrighteousness." Proverbs 16:9 reads, "A man's heart deviseth his way: but the Lord directeth his steps."

She did not understand how this related to all of the other Scripture that was reveled to her. The last verse given to her, Acts 2:17, reads, "And it shall come to pass in the last days, saith God, I will pour out my Spirit upon all flesh: and your sons and daughters shall prophesy, and your young men shall see visions, and your old men shall dream dreams:"

"Why was this verse given to me, Lord? I cannot make the connection with all of the other Word you gave me! I can somewhat see Your direction in the others. I can see how this is Divine Word that You are leading me to share with Matthew. Elizabeth then fell to her knees and began to pray ardently.

"Heavenly Father, thank you for all of the blessings that you have given me. Thank you for Your grace, mercy, and love. Thank you for an enjoyable evening at the party. It was a joy to be able to have a conversation with Matthew and be able to talk about You with him, as well. Father, I cannot see how all of the Scripture that You have given me will work for Matthew, but You know what is best! Please open his eyes to see these truths or reveal insight to him that I may be able, with Your help, to answer his questions or calm his concerns. Show him tonight, Lord, while it is still on his mind and still weighing heavily in his heart. I know that You have a purpose for his life, just as You do for mine. Please help him to see that he has an important role to play in the advancement of Your Kingdom! Thank you, Father, for hearing my requests, and for always walking with me, and for loving and protecting me. And thank you for bringing Matthew into my life! I know that we cannot start a relationship until he surrenders his heart to You. For You tell me in Your Holy Word in II Corinthians 6:14 that we cannot be a couple. I do not even know if he has come into my life for this reason. I do know that I felt comfortable and relaxed with him, Father. I felt safe. I know that he would never dishonor or shame me, despite what rumors I have heard about him in the past. I see the heart of a loving, compassionate, and passionate man. I know that You made him that way. If there is a future for us, I know it is in Your hands and that You already know if it is to be. No matter what, my life is for Your glory; my love for You will not change either way. But I thank you for allowing me to enjoy time with a man without the pressure of 'a date.' Give Matthew strength, Father, because the questions that are assuredly going through his mind tonight are going to cause unrest. Let him experience the peace that knowing You will bring. Thank you, for allowing me just to continue to talk as I have. I give You all the praise and glory, in Jesus name, Amen!"

Elizabeth arose from the floor, and climbed into bed. Before she turned out her lamp, she paused and looked towards the ceiling, as if she was staring up into space. She briefly closed her eyes, nodded her head in approval, and smiled. She relaxed her head into the soft pillow, knowing that Matthew was going to be all right.

Seven

Meanwhile, as this was going on at Elizabeth's apartment, Matthew was arriving at his apartment as well. He had just parked his car in the garage at his apartment and was walking towards the elevator when his cell phone rang.

Matthew wondered, "Who would be calling me at this hour?" He looked at the caller ID to reveal that it was his sister, Mandy. "Oh, God, I hope nothing is wrong! She never calls this late!" He allowed his mind to feverishly race through scenarios: is it Mom? Is it Dad? Did she have an accident?" Hurriedly, he flipped open his phone and hastily inquired, "Mandy! Is everything okay? What's wrong?"

Mandy put his fears to rest immediately, answering him in her calm and reassuring voice, "Calm down, brother! Everyone is fine! Mom went to bed hours ago and Dad just went to bed a little while ago! He fell asleep in his recliner watching the television again! Hey, I'm sorry to be calling you at this hour. I know you are probably still at the Omega, but I just need to talk to you! Can you call me when you leave? I don't care what time it is. It is very important that I talk to you tonight, um, I mean, before you go to bed!"

Matthew informed her, "I've already left the hotel. In fact, I am in the garage and I was walking towards the elevator when you called! What do I owe the pleasure of this call?"

Mandy paused before answering, "I just really needed to talk to you! I have been upset all evening!"

Matthew concernedly asked, "Mandy, honey, what's wrong? What can I do to help?

Mandy assured him, "I'm fine! I am doing great in school; yeah, it's hard, and the tests that are approaching rather rapidly are going to be among the hardest that I have ever experienced! This call is about you!"

Matthew was now confused. "Did I forget a birthday or an anniversary?" Matthew began to scroll through dates in his mind. "I cannot think of any important dates! What did I do? Did I forget to do something? Did I promise you anything?"

"Relax, Matt!" Mandy giggled. "Your memory is still intact, for now anyway! You *are* getting older, you know!" After she had finished with her laughter, her tone changed to become very reserved. "Hey, big brother, you know how much I love you don't you?"

Matthew felt a warm feeling begin to swallow up his heart. "Yes, I think so. Do you know how much I love you?"

Mandy responded, "Yes, I do big brother! You know that I always listen to you when you offer me advice. I really respect your insight and your life experience lessons that you can share with me. However, tonight is the rare opportunity that I get to share some advice with you. Promise me that you will hear me out, keep an open mind, and not interrupt me until I have finished!"

Matthew's demeanor became morose. He somehow sensed what she was going to talk to him about. "I promise. You know that I always listen to you!"

Mandy interjected, "Matt, I have been sensing uncomfortable things in my spirit all evening and into the night;

that is why I had to call you. Is everything all right, I mean, really?"

"Tonight was, let's just say, different. I met a young woman who reminds me so much of you!" Matthew informed her. "I think you would like her!"

"Really? What is her name? What do you know about her?" Mandy asked swiftly. "Is she pretty?"

"Her name is Elizabeth Angel. She raises money for a non-profit organization that builds schools, churches, and probably everything else in underdeveloped countries. And, yes, she is beautiful; and she is smart, too, but not as smart as you!" Matthew informed.

"See, I told you that your 'angel' would come along some day when you least expect it! Mandy joked. "When did you meet her? I thought your date's name was, uh, Nicole, was it?"

"Yes, you are correct. I met Elizabeth at the party. I really didn't feel like having conversations with the 'alpha' class of the year, and Nicole wanted to meet as many people as she could; therefore, I excused myself to the bar to get a drink, and that is when, well, the rest is history. We just started talking. She could care less who I am or how successful I am; I mean she cares about who I am, but not what I am. It was so relaxing and refreshing to have an intelligent conversation with a woman that could care less about the society page in *The Times* or was too busy playing model all evening." Matthew could talk endlessly it seemed about Elizabeth. This surprised him...and warmly excited him as well.

Hey, what happened to Nicole? Did you ditch her? That would be seriously rude and so unlike you!" Mandy chided.

Matthew smiled. "No, I didn't 'ditch her', as you so eloquently phrased it. She approached me while I was talking to Elizabeth"-

Mandy interrupted, "Ooh, was she jealous? Was she angry with you? Gosh, I would have loved to have been there to see that!"

"No on all counts! She was very friendly when I introduced her to Elizabeth! Actually, she broke her date with me!" Matthew informed her.

"Come on! I know that you cannot be serious! Brother, you've got some explaining to do!" Mandy answered.

"When she came over to our table, she had asked Elizabeth if she would excuse me for a moment, to which she graciously obliged. Once Nicole had me privately, she informed me that she had met a photographer who was in high demand in Manhattan now, and that he had a cancellation later that night. He was leaving the party to do a photo shoot then, and after that Nicole could accept the vacant appointment if she so desired. She accepted before asking me, but she was sincere when she asked if it was okay if she broke our date. She promised that she would make it up to me, but I doubt if I will ever hear from her again. Especially if her photo shoots, her portfolio, or whatever else models need, gets in the hand of any of the agencies. She will not have time to socialize," Matthew explained.

"So, you spent the evening with Elizabeth?" Mandy asked "Yes. It was a wonderful evening, at least until she left"-

"You chased off two women tonight?" Mandy queried Matthew.

Matthew continued, "If you would let me finish, I will tell you what happened! After Nicole left, Elizabeth and I spent another two hours talking before she excused herself to go home. She had a car waiting and had been waiting over an hour when she left. She wanted to get some sleep before she goes to church this morning! Hey, what about you? Don't you need to get some sleep before you go to church?"

"You are forgetting; I am used to being up for long periods of time!" Mandy reminded him. "Do you remember the killer rotations I had at the hospitals? This is a piece of cake. So, Elizabeth is a Christian? What was she doing at a party like that?"

"She was being recognized for her fundraising efforts and all the construction that was completed due to the money she collected. She could not see the point in her attendance, either," Matthew explained as he was stepping off the elevator. Walking to his apartment door, he continued. "Yes, I can say with all confidence and certainty, that Elizabeth is a firm believer in her faith."

Mandy paused. "Good for you! I should say good for Elizabeth! My brother is quite a catch! He just needs honed on his rough edges, though! Well, maybe that is my confirmation that calling you was the right thing to do! Remember you promised you would listen to me without interrupting!"

"I have been listening to you!" Matthew insisted. He laid his keys on the kitchen counter and continued with his thought, "What is it that has you calling me at this hour and has you upset as well? I do not like it when you are troubled!"

"I have been concerned about you, Matt. I have been sensing in my spirit that you are on the threshold of a life altering decision or experience of some kind. Do you know that I still pray for you every morning and night? I want to have my brother in Heaven with me as well as here on earth!" Mandy confessed.

"What happened? Was today designated as 'Attack Matthew with Religion Day?'" Matthew asked incredulously.

"Why are you upset already, Matt? I have not said a word! You promised"-

Matthew interrupted his sister again, "First it was Elizabeth and now you! Man, she really *does* remind me a lot of you!"

Mandy was stunned; she smiled, shook her head as if in disbelief, and then continued, "What did Elizabeth say to you? I like this woman already! I am even more amazed that you spent the evening talking to her! Was it the conversation or was it her?"

"It was a little bit of both, actually," Matthew confessed. "She was saying things about Christianity and the Bible in a way that I cannot recall ever hearing it defined before. Do you remember when we were growing up? Do you ever remember hearing our old bag-of-bones pastor ever talking about love? I only remember him talking about 'tarrying 'till Jesus comes', or his 'fire and brimstone' sermons; you know, always telling us to repent of our sins, and how Jesus died for us. I don't remember him talking much about how much God *loves* us, or reminding us that God is still alive! Elizabeth got me reeled in by causing a debate; she almost made it seem like I was arguing a court case, which, by the way, she would make a fine attorney, herself! She was a formidable opponent! I would hate to go up against her everyday! I mean, in a court of law! I can't explain it; she made it interesting. I had to hear her explanation of things. I wanted to know her theory. She sounds a lot like you!"

Mandy boasted, "That is because we both believe in the same God! He is the one true God; the One that sent His only son to die for you and me to pay for our transgressions!"

Matthew sighed, "Okay, enough on this subject for one day! Now why did you *really* call me?"

Mandy persisted, "This is why I called you, Matt! I told you... I just feel it so strongly in my spirit that you are about to undergo a terrifying ordeal! I wanted to warn you so that you would have your defenses on guard! I wanted you to be ready for anything unusual, so in the event that it does happen, you will be ready!"

"I love you, Mandy, more than any brother ever loved his sister, but I am having a little trouble deciphering all of this that I have been inundated with tonight! Please be a little more patient with me! This is too much of a coincidence; to be presented with similar scenarios twice in the same day, it's almost surreal."

Matthew asked, almost pleadingly, "Sis, whatever is going on has me genuinely concerned. I know that you believe all of this Spiritual stuff; I know that Elizabeth does, too. I'm just not ready to pursue this further until I know more! Just please continue to pray and put in a good word for me, will you?"

"Why do you make everything have to be a case of law? You always need tangible evidence! Let me ask you this. How do you know that you love me?" Mandy asked.

The absurdity of the question stunned Matthew. "I know it! I always have; even when we had our little disagreements or scuffles, I never was mad enough not to love you…ring your neck, maybe, but- what kind of a question is that?"

"It is a very serious question, Matt! *How* do you know you love me? Can you see it? Can you touch it? What evidence do you have to prove what you say is true?" Mandy interrogated further.

"I do not need any evidence! I know it in my heart!" Matthew exclaimed, pounding his chest with his free hand.

Mandy continued, "Well, how do you know it is real without any visible proof? How do I know?"

Matthew was becoming weary with the questions. Matthew answered emphatically, "You have to believe me! You cannot be serious! Do you have doubts about it? Please, Mandy, believe me, trust me, with all of my heart, I love you! You have been my closest friend!"

Mandy softly and reassuringly consoled him, "That is what it is all about, big brother! The foundation of being a Christian is trust! Our faith, you have to believe and trust the Bible and the promises that are in it! The promises are for you, too, Matt!"

Matthew tenderly asked, "Will you please call me tomorrow, maybe we can talk more? Suddenly, I'm very tired. I need to rest and try to sort out everything that has happened today."

Mandy smiled. Her face began to radiate a new shade of warmth. "You bet! I will call you first thing after church! I love you, Matt!"

"Good night, Mandy," Matthew wished. He closed his phone, walked over to his bedside table and placed it by his lamp. His mind was lost in all of the things said to him tonight (and this morning) by Elizabeth and Mandy. He was beginning to get a headache. He felt ill; no, he was not getting sick, it was a hollow feeling inside him. It was slowly enveloping his insides. He wanted to forget this past twelve hours; but at the same time, he wants to relive almost every moment. He loves his long talks with his sister. She always relaxed him. He could escape from reality for a few moments; it was just the two of them whenever they talked. The needs and concerns that they each had and shared were all that really mattered in those brief, fleeting moments. Now it was Elizabeth. She was unlike any woman that he had ever met; she was unlike *anyone* he had ever met. She was confident, trusting; she was secure with herself and sure of herself. However, the one thing he could not understand was her assurance *within* herself. This was causing the war that was raging within him. He was envious of her. When it became about herself as a person, she was at peace with ...and within. He wondered what it would feel like to experience life in that manner for a day. Oh, he is confident; he is sure of himself, but something was missing. He thought, before tonight anyway, that he was happy. He was almost despondent as he realized that the things that Mandy and Elizabeth possessed, that he wanted, were peace and joy. The effervescence within flowed out whenever they would speak; you could see it in their eyes, and you could see it in their countenance. You know they are special. Yes, he has met others that have struck him as odd, not weird, psychotic or anything, just different, mind you. It is just that Mandy meant something to him; he was close to her. Maybe, he thought to himself, that is why it is so noticeable to him. Why is it so easy to see the same in Elizabeth? He had just met her, but it seemed rather obvious that she possessed the same traits as Mandy. He wanted a drink, but he wanted a clear mind more. Perhaps the best thing to do would be to go to bed and reconvene his thoughts here after a good night's sleep. He walked into his bathroom, brushed his teeth, put on a sweatshirt, a pair of lounge pants, and a pair of slippers then lumbered into his bedroom. After sitting down on the edge of his bed, he took off his slippers, took a drink of a bottle of water that was on the table, and turned off the light. As he lay back in his bed, he told himself that all he needed was to just clear his mind, not entertain any thoughts of any kind, and just relax and go to sleep. Relax. Matthew somehow knew that it was going to be easier to say than do on this night.

Eight

Matthew's mind was full with many things. He was thinking about home, Mom and Dad, his sister Mandy, and Elizabeth; *especially* Elizabeth and the conversation that they had shared. He pondered aloud. "I know that there is a God. I know that he is real. I have the evidence in Mandy. I suppose I can say that the same is true of Elizabeth. If it is not spiritual or of God, then I cannot say what it could be. Why do I feel as if I am only living to die? Why do I sometimes feel as if I am going through the motions, and just trying to survive this jungle day to day? God, if You are listening to me, I need answers! Show me something, anything that will help me with this encumbrance that is on my mind so heavily!"

Matthew walked over to look out his window. He had not yet closed his vertical blinds, and even at 2:00 AM, there are plenty of lights to see. The sky was clear, but you could not see the stars. That is what he missed from home. Matthew lowered his head in disappointment. That is why he took a picture that he and Mandy had taken one night many years ago; one of the most beautiful night skies he could remember, and had it air brushed onto his blinds. When they are closed, he is back in New Hope with Mandy, looking up at that big purple sky all aglow with millions of stars. Even when they are closed, there is light from the city that contrives its way into his room by encompassing the window frame and exudes itself on the walls around it. Matthew stared at this scenery for a few more seconds, looked heavenward as if he was waiting on someone to speak to him, and then sighed heavily. He briskly rubbed his head, turned off his cell phone, and walked toward his bed. He had not begun this day with plans to be alone tonight, but it did not upset him that he was. He had too much to think about to entertain thoughts of any possible interaction tonight. Besides, he is still thinking about Elizabeth. Could there be a future with her? She did not seem to care about my money, or money in general. She was comfortable with herself; she saw no need to change her appearance to impress anyone. He liked that. It was refreshing in a city of nip and tuck, enlargements, botox injections, and liposuction. She is perfect just as she is. He sat down on the edge of his bed and thought even more. Why did he meet her? Why was she at this party? Why did Nicole get a career opportunity during the party, and end our date? Not that he was complaining; it was just another in a series of questions that had inundated his mind the past several minutes. Moreover, he still was seeking a response or a sign; something from God to acknowledge that He has heard him. Once again, Matthew exhaled a deep sigh. He leaned over towards the table beside his bed, looked around the room as if he was expecting someone, and not finding anyone turned off the light and fell into bed. The room still had a glow from the lights of the city that lingered around his windows. It was just enough escaping the top to allow him to see the stars on his blinds as they were when he was at home in New Hope.

"New Hope", Matthew thought aloud. "Why did Elizabeth say that Mandy and I represent that to many people-new hope. I never thought of my job as that. A second chance, maybe. Mandy, well, I always thought of her as a miracle worker. Maybe even an angel on earth. She is definitely a very successful doctor in the making. That is precisely what I am looking for now, new hope. I want to experience true happiness- true joy. Am I still hiding my fear from 9/11 by trying to be the seemingly selfless, cold-hearted S.O.B. people think I am? Who am I, really? What have I made myself? Millions of people would trade places with me in a nanosecond, so what reasons do I have to complain? I do not have any wants or needs, materially speaking. If I want it, I can go buy it. Money is no object. But I still feel so hollow, shallow, and even empty. Ah, I'm only kidding myself! The answers I want are not coming tonight, that's for sure! I don't think that God is going to make a house call to *me* at this time of night, uh, morning. That is for people like Mandy and Elizabeth. Maybe there is a place and purpose for me. But right now, it's here in this bed." Matthew then groaned loudly, "I do not want to go to the office this morning! Just once, I would love to sleep in and just say 'to hell with it!' The world will survive for one day if I did not show up! Maybe I will take off a day! I need more time for me! I need to relax, and think more about the things that are weighing on my mind!" Having decided this, Matthew then closed his eyes, fluffed his pillows, then rolled over to go to sleep. He is prepared to sleep in. He even remembered to turn off his alarm clock. *Nothing* is going to stop him from enjoying a good night's sleep now! Little did he know, that whenever you say, 'I will never', you do. And when you say, 'Nothing can happen', it does. Plans are always subject to change. Matthew was about to see a drastic change in his plans very soon.

Matthew abruptly awakened from a sound and relaxing sleep feeling very apprehensive. What awakened him from his sleep? How long had he been asleep? He was still tired. It felt as if it were only minutes ago that he had gone to bed. He was about to roll over and return to sleep when he realized that the glow from the city lights were no longer outlining his windows. The light from his clock was off, as well. Ugh! A power outage has befallen upon the city! He groggily wondered what caused this one. As he got out of bed to walk to the window to see if there were any evidence of the cause, he realized that the floor felt different. Not in a strange way, mind you, but different; warmer than usual, especially with a power outage. When he got to the window, he was astonished to see that his blinds were now open. In fact, there were no blinds there at all! Everything was black; Matthew could not remember it ever being this black outside, not even in New Hope! He could not even recognize the buildings that were adjacent to his apartment building through this cloud of darkness!

"No problem," Matthew thought. "I'll just grab my cell phone and make a couple calls and learn what has happened."

As Matthew walked back to the table, he was becoming increasingly concerned of the warmth radiating from his floor. He reached down to pick up his phone, only to discover that the display flashed a message stating, "No service".

"Great!" Matthew mumbled. "What if something were to really happen?" Matthew thought about what he just said. Wait a minute! Is it possible that something "*really happened*" already? Matthew started to feel a twinge of anxiety churning in his stomach. As he turned to approach the windows, Matthew realized that the room was different. He must have somehow turned around unawares to him, because he now cannot find the windows! As he paced around aimlessly in the darkness, he realized that his bedside table was not where he thought it was, and his bed as well! He also realized that the floor was maintaining its warmth. Was it getting hotter? It seemed as if it were. His mind was beginning to play havoc on his senses. Logic and common sense assured him that he was in his room; he was just temporarily incoherent. That is what it *had* to be! Wait! What is that smell? Is it sulfur?

"Oh my God, the building is on fire!" Matthew panicked in his mind. Suddenly, a rational thought permeated the panic. Wait a minute. There were no buildings nearby with electricity when he looked out the window, and there was no glow of fire from his building. There are no people screaming in the hallway. There is not even a sound! No sound; why is that? There is no electricity anywhere to see and there is no sound! There are no fire trucks or police cars piercing the silence with the screaming of their sirens, nobody panicking in the streets, nobody is doing *anything*! Matthew has now since gone back to feeding the panic that was growing at an alarming rate. Now he was trying to use his intellect to solve the terrifying conundrum that has befallen around him.

"I'm dreaming! This is all a dream! That is the only thing that makes any sense at this moment!" Then once again, Matthew regained clarity. "I cannot control a dream! This is real! Oh, God, what is going on?"

The smell of sulfur was slowly but steadily increasing. The floor was getting warmer, but still not too hot to continue to walk upon. Now the question is- to where is he walking? Matthew had many questions, but no answers. He began to think that he could die tonight. He started regretting the fact that he did not call his parents more often. He regretted the fact that he did not go home to visit more often. He regrets that he was not a better brother to Mandy; he could have been a much better son. He was regretting working too much and playing too little. Not all the money in property, stocks, bonds, IRAs, and bank accounts can save him from the fate that is awaiting him now.

Matthew had another disturbing thought. "What if there was another terrorist attack? What if we were bombed? Why didn't I hear it? How many others survived besides me? Why can't I hear *anything?* The silence is deafening! I haven't heard anything since I awakened into this nightmare!" He continued walking slowly towards the emptiness that was before him. He was still walking in blackness. It was as if he had gone blind. He cannot remember ever being this fearful. He continued moving forward with hopes of finding escape, answers, human life; he needed to find a flicker of hope.

It seemed as if he had been walking for hours. He was aware that he was no longer sleepy. At least it was something that allowed him to chuckle at himself. The silence, the darkness, the uncertainty were all things that acted like drugs; he felt as if he had been infused with caffeine and cocaine. He was so awake and aware of his situation he was now beginning to tremble involuntarily.

"What else can happen?" Matthew muttered to himself.

No sooner had this thought passed through his mind, he realized the floor was now not only hot, but it had also become craggy. He is now thankful for his house slippers; he also realizes that the stench of sulfur has now integrated with a malodorous aroma he cannot quite comprehend. Suddenly, he was able to interpret the new addition: it was the smell of burning flesh! People are being incinerated!

"What a ghastly way to die!" Matthew thought. He also began to realize that he too might meet his demise in the same manner. He was choking to grasp any fresh air he could breathe for his lungs. The ground was becoming more treacherous; not only was it becoming even hotter, the terrain was becoming rougher and there was something liquid now he could feel through his shoes. It was too thick for water; he could only fathom what this sludge may be. Matthew felt like crying and he felt like giving up. But if there were any chance of escaping from this hell, he knew that he had to continue. He was not ready to die yet; and he certainly did not plan to die in this manner!

Nine

Matthew was positive that he had been walking for miles by now. The muscles in his legs were burning; his feet were burning, too, but that was because of the heat from whatever it was that he was walking on. His eyes were desiccated; he was becoming increasingly thirsty, too. The smell had not become worse (as if it could get worse?), so Matthew took that as progress; a positive in this conspicuously negative situation. He continued to navigate his way forward when he noticed- the blackness was no longer impenetrable! The space before him was now a dark grey; he could tell that he was walking through profuse smoke, which was the source of his coughing and his burning eyes. With every step that he hobbled forward, he could see that the darkness was lifting slightly. With a new motivation and determination, Matthew increased, though ever slightly, his pace. He had no idea where he was walking to or what awaited him. He only knew that if he was going to die, he wanted to face it; he would rather see the flames that would engulf him rather than to die in the dark and be defeated by an unseen enemy. If he could see what he was battling, he could construct a plan; a plan to prolong life, or escape death, whichever he could achieve successfully.

"I wonder how many people will come to my funeral? I wonder if Elizabeth will come? Will they find enough of me to bury?" Matthew questioned aloud. He had to change his mindset. It was too negative! He has always been a positive thinker; even in the most bizarre circumstances, even in the worst-case scenarios when a pending litigation deemed hopeless, he was confident his skills would prevail. However, this was beyond bizarre; this was macabre! He wondered if this even remotely resembled the circumstances that the people in the Twin Towers experienced; his building was not crumbling to the ground and he was not yet able to see flames, so no, his situation is not even in the same league as theirs! It is amazing the things you think of when you are facing death; the things you never accomplished, the people you hurt, the people you loved, the absurdity of your selfish ambitions, and the chance of happiness you may have sacrificed to obtain the lofty career status you achieved. None of it mattered to him now. The only thing that matters is arriving at the end of this hellish impediment that is before him. The ground beneath his feet had now incorporated a slight incline; something similar to the handicap ramps you would see in a building for people in wheelchairs or with walkers.

"I wonder what's next!" Matthew uttered to himself. "Nothing would surprise me now!" After walking about one hundred yards after speaking those prophetic words, the *next thing* happened. The dark grey smoke was now light grey. He could see more than inches in front of him for the first time since this trek began! He could see that the path he was walking upon was narrow; it could not have been more than three feet wide. There was nothing but clouds of smoke on either side of the path, so he did not know how far the fall would be if he should falter and slip off the path.

"Since the smoke is clearing why don't you take some of the stench with it?" Matthew screamed into the emptiness. What was that? Was it an echo? Was his mind beginning to play games with him? Maybe it was stress. Maybe it was being alone in the total silence for so long. He was sure that he heard something.

"Hello! Is anyone there?" Matthew yelled. Again, he had faintly heard something directly ahead of him. "Maybe there is someone else trapped in this with me! Maybe I have reached the end of the destination! Why have I not heard this person or persons sooner?" Matthew was pondering several thoughts in his mind right now. He was becoming impatient. Why have they not answered him? "Hey! Can you hear me? Where are you?" he shouted aloud again. This time, the sound was louder, but still unintelligible. He began to increase his pace. He had to find the source of the sound he was hearing. Looking ahead, it looked as if the floor was moving. "It must be the smoke playing tricks with my eyes," Matthew thought. As he continued walking towards his hope of finding any other human trapped with him, he realized that his eyes were fine. He did see movement, but it was not the floor. He also realized he was no longer alone; well, technically, he was still alone. Whatever was there with him was not human; at least it was no more. As he continued walking this narrow corridor, the things that were moving along the floor began to grab at his feet. They were trying to prohibit his continuance on this journey to nowhere. It was slowing him down considerably, as he had to break the grips of these hindrances that were below him. He began to stomp them as he walked; however, this was only a temporary solution. As soon as Matthew became confident that he had solved his problem, a new one developed. They now had begun to clutch his ankles. That is when he realized what it was-human hands!

"Oh my God!" Matthew exclaimed. They were very strong. He realized that this struggle was going to be much more tedious...and treacherous. As he continued to free himself from the grasps of the hands that were clinging to his ankles or anything that they may seize as it passes by, he began to wonder if these people were trapped and trying to escape as well.

"Hey! Can anyone hear or understand me?" Matthew asked. The only reply that returned was a blood-curdling shriek that he could not define. Repugnant is the only way to describe it. There was no way that this could be happening; the smell of burning flesh, the lack of other human encounters, the repulsive screams that have now become more frequent; it was all something out of a good horror movie. This does not happen in real life.

"This has to be a dream! God, please let me wake up! I cannot take this anymore!" Matthew pleaded. He did not stop. He was too terrified to stop. He rationalized that if he stopped, he would become one of them, whatever they were, and he did not particularly want to stick around to find out. "Maybe it was something I ate or something I drank! Maybe it was drugs; someone must have spiked my drink when I was not looking!" Matthew began to speculate. The only people that could have tainted his drinks were the bartender or Elizabeth. He knew it could not have been either of them. Paranoia began to set in; what if Nicole had done this when they kissed? He had heard about this kind of thing before, even though he now thinks it was in a James Bond movie. Matthew was losing his edge. He was no longer as focused as he was before. This lapse in his clarity had allowed the hands to steal his shoes from his feet as he continued to scuttle his way through this myriad of dangers. Now barefoot, Matthew realized that he was walking on metal girding. He could feel heat all around him, but the metal was not hot. This jerked him back to his senses very quickly. He now had to decipher this riddle. However, he wondered…would he have enough time?

The metal was not hot, but it was rough, almost sharp.

The cut allowed for grip: traction, and sure-footedness as if for walking in inclement weather. However, this was not helping Matthew at all. He could feel the flesh on the bottom of his feet breaking. He could even feel his blood gently oozing from the lacerations as it mingled with the steel underneath them. Now he began to wonder about a possible new danger. "What if they can smell blood? Will that incite violence from these…things?" He suddenly acquired a seemingly great idea at the time. He ripped the sleeves from his pajamas and manipulated them to create makeshift coverings for his battered feet. Though it provided little protection, it, however, did provide some relief. Suddenly, he remembered his conversation with Mandy. "She had already known about this! She warned me that something was going to happen!" Matthew thought audibly to himself. "How did she know? Did God really tell her so that she could warn me?" he knew Mandy was not psychic; she did not believe in such things. She always said that it was of the devil if they actually had any power or merits. Otherwise, it was merely just someone who was predicting events, and if they did not come to pass, they would explain it away with some far-fetched cosmic theory. But now, he had to focus on his situation. She had told him it would be life altering. He was confident that this would classify as such an event.

Now that he could see somewhat, Matthew could now establish that his surroundings were changing. The floor was no longer the corrugated metal it once was; it was now like bricks. It was no longer warm, either. The odor was beginning to fade; he could finally breathe air that was, for lack of a better explanation, reminiscent of New York on a bad day. The 'things' that were tearing at him had vanished, as well. It now looked as if he were walking through storm clouds. It was still hard to see, but at least he could now walk with a purpose and not blindly and aimlessly as he was before on this journey. He felt his muscles begin to ease their tension.

He felt his whole body allow itself to relax for a moment. He was weary, but he was determined to reach some semblance of sanity on this pathway to…somewhere. The air continued to become lighter, clearer. It had been a long time since his lungs had inhaled a breath of life this fresh. He silently vowed never to take the city air for granted again. He also vowed to return home more often once this hallucination ends. Matthew now began to reason within himself. "I can now see if I were to be approached by anyone or anything. The ground is no longer burning my feet. There is no longer anything grabbing at me to hinder my walk. It may be safe for me to stop to rest perhaps for a moment! The air is clean, and I need to rest! I need to be sharp to allow me to focus on the task that is before me now and try to prepare for any situation that may present itself as I continue on this path." Now that he was convinced in his thoughts that it was safe to rest, Matthew allowed himself to lie down. Even though he was sitting on bricks, it felt good to be off of his feet for a moment or two. He removed his makeshift shoes and rubbed his weary, aching feet. As he inspected each one, he found them engulfed with scrapes, cuts, and gashes. His calves and ankles did not fare much better; it was evident that human fingernails made the scrapes and scratches. He has seen many examples from evidence exhibit photos presented during the may trials he was associated with over the years. His mind wanted to try to comprehend whatever was going on back there. Why were they there? Who were they? Where were they from? Probably the most important question, why didn't they answer him when he was trying to communicate with them or, to be more accurate, trying to communicate with anyone who would listen and would respond, anyone who *could* respond. Right now, he was too tired to worry about all of it. He was too tired to care. As he lied back on the unforgiving bricks, to him it was as welcome and as comfortable as any grassy knoll back in New Hope.

As he looked skyward, he could actually recognize clouds moving above him. The soothing sight relaxed his mind and his body. He closed his eyes, and found himself thanking God for this brief moment of tranquility. Almost instantly, Matthew drifted off into a peaceful and much needed sleep.

Ten

It seemed like only moments ago Matthew had fallen asleep. Now a firm, but tender push on his shoulder is awakening him.

"Matthew? Matthew! We need to go! It's time to wake up! You are already late! Matthew! Come on, now! If only you would have stayed at your original location, this would be going much more efficient!" the voice said.

Matthew was still trying to focus his eyes to see the face that accompanied the authoritative and strangely calming voice. "Who are you?" Matthew asked. As his focus became clear, he realized that the person standing over him was dressed in a white robe-like garment with a thin golden band engaged as a belt around the waist. His hair was blonde, but it was as if it were illuminated. His face was also illuminated, but he could determine that he was a rather young man, possibly in his early to mid-thirties. Since he still had not responded to the question, Matthew asked him again, "Who are you?"

"Matthew Craig, attorney from New York City, age thirty, single. Your mother and father still reside in New Hope, North Carolina. You also have a sister named Mandy, currently enrolled at Duke University School of Medicine. Is this correct?" the stranger asked.

"Yes, that's all correct. You know all about me. Now you can help me please by telling me who you are!" Matthew calmly responded.

"I'm sorry, but I'm afraid that I cannot tell you that!" the stranger replied. "You see, we are not permitted to tell the subjects our names. The only thing I can tell you is that the high court appointed me to ensure that you reach your appointment safely and promptly. However, when you went off on your little expedition, you may have prohibited me from accomplishing the latter. You nearly prevented the former all by yourself! Why did you leave your position? What were you thinking?"

Matthew could not believe his eyes. Is this an angel with whom he is having this conversation? He had seen pictures over the course of his life; most times, they also had halos, as well. This 'angel' did not. And what did he mean when he stated that I had left my position? Trying to make conversation with the young man, Matthew queried, "So, where is your halo? Have you not earned yours yet? Will my tardiness delay your promotion?"

"We don't have halos. That is a secular ideology; your kind invented that centuries ago through your artists' renderings of what an angel looks like." The man replied.

"So you are an angel!" Matthew exclaimed, as if he had just solved a mystery. "What was my position? When did I leave it? Tell me, just what in God's name are you talking about?"

"I suppose you can say that I am an angel, although that is not my title," the man replied. "Your position is our original determined starting point, your initial extraction point. You know, for a man that is unsure of God, you are confident when you talk about Him!"

"How do you know that about me? Wait; is that in your little file, too? What else do you know about me?" Matthew asked.

The angel responded, "Your file is not what I would consider 'little'. I only know what they have entrusted to me at this time. That is all that I need to know to transport you to your appointment."

Matthew persisted, "You still have not answered my question! What was my original position? Are you talking about my apartment? Hey, I don't know what happened, but I was not staying there! There was smoke, and I could feel heat, as if from a fire. My cell phone did not have service, and I could not stay there to die in those conditions!"

"I should have known! Your file has all the pertinent information I would need to bring you back; it's just that nobody *ever* leaves his or her position! They are over-whelmed with fear or surrender; he or she is always too terri-fied to leave their surroundings. They do not venture further into the unknown! You are a brave and bold man! I sense a proud man, as well. That always leads to defeat!" the angel declared.

"Hey, I'm sorry if I caused you to be late," Matthew admitted.

The angel tried to reassure Matthew. "Oh, you won't be late. No one is ever late for their appointment"-

"But you just said that"- Matthew interrupted.

"If you would let me finish, I will tell you!" The angel interrupted in kind. "You are never late for your appoint-ment! We like to get people there early to allow themselves time to absorb the enormity of their situation; we know that their minds will not be able to comprehend the images of the surroundings and the sounds that they are about to witness. It is too much for the finite, human mind to ascertain!"

"Where is my appointment?" Matthew asked somberly.

"You will see. We will be there in a moment," the angel replied.

Matthew was now beginning to feel nauseous; he did not like uncertainty, and the surprises that arise along with it. He noticed that his surroundings were becoming much sharper, much clearer. He could see a brightening blue sky, camouflaged by a plethora of thick, white clouds that looked like giant pieces of cotton. It seemed as if the sky was becoming brighter with every step. He also noticed the silhouette of what appeared to be a building emitting from the clouds on the horizon. He was very uncomfortable with his situation. He was always in control; he was at the mercy of unknowns, and he could not function with unknowns. That is why he relentlessly attacked them in his profession. He always prepared for any circumstance that could possibly present itself in the courtroom, and eliminated each one with deft, craftiness, and knowledge. This occasion he had no idea what to prepare for. Although he could now clearly see his surroundings, he felt as if he was flying blind. Matthew looked towards the angel for a moment and asked, "How much longer before we are there?"

"Look forward," answered the angel. "You have arrived".

Matthew gasped as if all the oxygen had escaped his lungs. The building that had been hiding within the clouds minutes earlier was now before him. Actually, it was a stairway leading to what appeared to be an enormous judge's bench. There were massive white pillars along the steps on each side and encompassing the back of the structure that was before him. There were additional seats, slightly offset, on either side of the judge's seat, but it was evident that they were not for witnesses, as the only way to approach them was from behind. The brightness of the light from behind the judge's chair was so brilliant that you would almost think that the sun was residing there. He could not tell if anyone was sitting there or not. Seconds seemed like hours. After what must have been several minutes, or so it seemed to Matthew, he could not withhold the barrage of questions any longer.

"What is this all about?" Matthew asked.

"You will see at the appointed time," the angel replied.

"If I have an appointment, and I did not stay in my room as you say that I should have, are you telling me that my wait would have been even longer?" Matthew continued his query.

"As I told you, the time was to allow you a chance to prepare for all this before you," the angel quickly responded. "Do you wish you had that time now?"

"I wish I could have avoided the assault that I took along my endeavor! Some of those will leave scars! Thank goodness there are no serious burns!" Matthew exclaimed.

"How are you feeling, Matthew?" the angel asked.

Matthew looked puzzled by the question. "What do you mean, how do I feel? I am on the verge of losing my mind. I am not prepared for this meeting, appointment, or whatever this is!"

The angel continued to press, "How do you feel physically? Are your feet hurting? What about your legs and arms?"

"Now that you mention it, I feel fine, actually," Matthew answered bewilderingly as he rubbed his arms. "Hey! My arms are completely healed!" He began inspecting his calves, ankles, and feet. "My legs are healed, too! How did that happen? When did this happen?"

The angel was feeling sorrowful for Matthew. "Why is it so hard for you to believe?"

"Believe what?" Matthew asked him, still amazed at the disappearance of all his injuries.

"Never mind," the angel sighed. "You will find out what I mean very soon!"

"What time is it anyway? Is it still Sunday? How long will my appointment take to complete?" Matthew continued with his questioning.

"I would not know the answer to any of your questions; we do not monitor time as you do, and each appointment is different," the angel explained.

Matthew could not believe his ears! "How do you know what time my appointment begins? How do you know I didn't already miss it because of my unscheduled endeavor? How can you have order if you do not know the time?" Matthew asked incredulously.

"It is all in His control! You will see!" the angel assured him.

Matthew continued looking at the massive bench. "Man, I wonder what it would be like to take part in a trial in this court!" he thought to himself, but it resonated in his ears as if he had said it out loud. While he was still pondering that dilemma, he could see that the sky around the judge's bench was growing rapidly dim. He could also see the emergence of what appeared to be a massive wrap-around screen; it was like something you would see at a theatre or even an auditorium. He was now beginning to become very anxious. "I'm really not in the mood to watch a movie! I just want to"-

He glanced to his right to the spot that the angel once occupied, only to find it now was vacant. "Go... home!" Matthew said, finishing his proclamation.

Eleven

Matthew stared at the blackness ahead of him. It seemed as if moments had passed since he last spoke, but it was merely seconds. He did not like the silence; it was deafening. He tended to become uneasy during the periods of silence. On his best day, he could not have imagined the magnitude in which the silence is about to be interrupted. Rather brusquely, a loud and resounding voice pierced the silence.

"How do you plead?" asked the mysterious voice.

The enormity of the voice distressed Matthew. Each word sounded like thunder, and bolts of white-hot lightning stretched its abundant tentacles, filling the sky and illuminating the room as the words echoed through the chamber. It is evident that he is in his domain, but also painfully evident that he is out of his jurisdiction. Matthew answered somewhat assertively, "What are the charges against me?"

"There are no charges being brought against you. How do you plead?" The inauspicious voice replied.

Matthew chuckled absurdly. "If there are no charges against me, then tell me why am I here?" he asked demandingly.

"Your life has brought you here!" the voice bellowed. The voice continued to sound as thunder, and the lightning continued to obey by responding to every word. The entire state of affairs was beginning to become overwhelming.

"I am sorry, but I do not understand! If I am not being charged, and it is my life that has brought me here, then basically what you are saying is that my life is on trial?" Matthew began to be an attorney despite his circumstances. It was inevitable. He is what he is. "So I am on trial for living?"

"YOU have brought the judgment against you!" The voice shouted with authority and conviction. "YOU lived your life without constraints! YOU had free will to choose your destiny. YOU had free will to choose your eternity! Again, I ask you, how do you plead?"

Matthew was now starting to comprehend the enormity of his situation. He was beginning to remember the conversations with Mandy concerning a day of judgment. He remembered her mentioning 'free will' several times to him when they spoke. Suddenly, another thought rushed through his mind. Was he dead? How did he die? He cannot remember any events that give evidence to support his death.

"It is not for you to know everything, Matthew! Some things happen when you are asleep; some things happen in the blink of an eye!" was the reply Matthew heard to his unspoken questions.

The voice seemingly knew his thoughts. He could not ask him forthright; he wanted to go an indirect route. But that would not be his style; that would not mirror his personality. So, in typical Matthew Craig fashion, he simply asked, "May I please ask who you are?"

Again the voice replied with authority, "You have heard me called I am! I have several names! You have heard some of them: EL, EL ELYON, ADONI, IMMANUEL, JEHOVAH, EL OLAM, ELOHIM, YHWH, YAH; but I believe you know be best as GOD! Are you ready to proceed?"

Matthew fell to his knees and buried his face between his outstretched arms. "Lord, I do not think I am, but we're going to continue anyway, aren't we?"

"You would be correct," God replied. "Matthew, rise up and watch the screens that are before you!"

Matthew rose to his feet as told, and immediately began to tremble. He was not in control of a situation for the first time in several years. What was about to transpire? What was going to appear on the screens? He cannot remember the last time he was so beleaguered. He felt as if he had concrete, or maybe even lead, upon his feet. He could not move. His feelings were surreal. It's like when you pass a car wreck. You really don't want to see it, but once you are there, you have to look. Thus, you know his feelings towards the gargantuan screens that were before him. He didn't want the element of surprise to be the victor in this trial, but he had a hint of impetuousness in his system that wanted to witness whatever it was he had to see.

The screens seemed to obtain power. There was a thick, smoky cloud that seemed to billow around them. As the clouds started to dissipate, he could see an image coming into focus. It appeared to be a hospital operating room; well, not a typical operating room. This was different. When he studied the scene closer, he realized that it was a birthing room! Someone was having a baby! Suddenly, he heard a woman screaming in pain. When the camera angle changed, he could now see the face of the woman lying in her bed.

It was his mother! She looked as he remembered her as a child. Could it be…wait a minute! He was watching his own birth! His mother looked disheveled; her hair was drenched with sweat. Every few minutes, she would allow a heart-stopping, blood-curdling scream to escape from the depths of her lungs. This went on for hours; Matthew was becoming visibly ill from watching his mother suffer so much and for such a prolonged time. She went through hell to allow him to be born. After one final push, he saw his mother's body fall lifelessly into the bed. She was exhausted beyond exhaustion. But she still managed to smile. She also somehow managed to find the strength to be able to hold that newborn baby boy when they placed him in her tired and aching arms. That baby was he. The smile was for him. That was a face he remembers seeing so much as a child, and really, through most of his life. Mom was, and still is, so full of love; she was proud to experience the culmination of this moment. He suddenly felt closer than ever to his mother; the love he was feeling was indescribable and unfathomable. He had nearly forgotten how beautiful his mother was when she was a young woman. However, he simultaneously felt humiliated and most unworthy because he did not show her more respect as he grew older. He did not deserve her love. She did not deserve the pain and heartaches that he has caused her over the years.

"Mothers forgive and forget easily, Matthew! That's why they are so special!" God replied; His voice shattered the silence.

"How did he know what- I mean, how did He, I didn't ask..." Matthew was thinking to himself.

"Because I can hear your thoughts as well as your words, Matthew; however, you knew that already!" God reminded him authoritatively.

Matthew's mind was racing; he could not comprehend the events that were transpiring before his eyes. In the past, he has represented several clients who had cases that seemed utterly hopeless; he was feeling the same about himself now. However, he does not know how to proceed with his current situation. This is a completely different circumstance and a completely different court; this one he does not know all the legalese terminology to allow him to extract himself from the state of affairs that he is now facing.

Matthew made an abrupt return to reality as he realized the image on the magnificent screens was changing. He was now looking at himself as an infant; he was in his back-yard, and his mother was pulling weeds from her flowers. As infants do, he began to crawl around in the yard but never out of his mother's sight. He watched what seemed to be trivial; his mother would occasionally wipe the sweat from her brow and continue with her weeding. He watched himself flop back on his butt when he would find something interesting in the yard, such as a bright yellow dandelion. Of course, even Matthew was a typical child, and was curious to how everything tasted; so, yes, after picking it out of the yard, it was time to eat. But before it made it to his lips, mother was there to take it away.

She did not scold him or get angry; she simply tossed it aside, smiled and gazed directly into Matthew's eyes and told him, "No!", with love but with authority. She then picked a dandelion that was ready to blow in the wind, and showed Matthew how much fun it is to blow them into the air. He seemed to approve, as he slapped his hands onto the ground repeatedly and emitted a gaggle of giggles that made Matthew laugh aloud as he watched.

This was fun for a little while, and infant Matthew became bored again, so he began to crawl through his personal jungle to seek another adventure. He saw something move in the grass; the thick and lush blades hid it as it moved, and Matthew wanted to see what this was! He crawled a little faster due to his excitement. He was almost able to see something else to do while mommy was busy.

But Matthew watched the screen in horror as he could see that he was crawling too fast upon a copperhead snake! He doesn't remember this! Why didn't his mother ever tell him about this? At that moment, the telephone began to ring. Matthew stopped crawling and mother stopped weeding. She brushed herself off quickly, walked over to Matthew, bent down, and picked him up to carry him into the house with her as she answered the phone call.

"Hello?" she asked the caller with her soft, warm voice.

"Hi, Honey!" was the reply on the other line. It was his father, Jacob.

"Hi, Daddy!" Mom replied. Since Mathew was born, and until this day, whenever Dad would call and either of us kids were around, she always called him daddy; on the phone around the house, it didn't matter. I think the only time he ever got to hear his name was in church, at work, or whenever Mom was upset. "It's the middle of the day! You hardly ever call from work! Is something wrong? Are you okay?"

"Stop with all the questions, my love! Everything here on my end is fine! I was calling you to see if everything was okay!" Jacob replied. "I was walking down on the main floor about ten minutes ago and I got this overbearing spirit on me that something was wrong at home. Well, I ignored it at first, thinking if something was wrong you would have called, so I just dropped it. But the further I walked, the stronger the urge to call became! My mind was racing now! I was thinking things like, 'What if they can't call? Who else could I call to check on you all if you did not answer the phone?' you know, crazy thoughts! But as soon as I started dialing our number, the depressing spirit left just as fast as it had come upon me! So, everyone is okay?"

Natalie reassured him, "Yes, everyone here is just fine! I am sure that it happened for a reason; it may have even been protection for you at the plant! We may never know the reason the Lord does some things! It was good to hear your voice honey. I love you, daddy! And Matthew does, too!"

"I love you all very much! I'll see you when I get home!" Jacob replied, and then he hung up the telephone and returned to work. He was smiling now. He was smiling for several reasons. He was glad that his family was safe;

he loved hearing Natalie's voice, even if it was on the telephone; he was also glad that he was obedient to the prompting of the Lord to call home. He received peace the instant he was obedient to the urging of the Spirit, and he received a blessing for his obedience. "God is so good to me and my family", Jacob thought to himself.

Matthew was amazed and bewildered as he watched the events that played out before him. He was afraid to watch, but he couldn't turn his eyes away from the movie that was his life. He had no idea what would appear next. He was receiving a history lesson on his early years. The next few hours would have seemed rather ho-hum to Matthew; it was just normal kid and family stuff; you know, playing, family meals, going to church, and saying his bedtime prayers. Mom and Dad were always encouraging him to pray. They were staunch believers in the power of prayers. He thought he was hearing his voice under the words he was speaking on the scenes as they played. He thought, "Man, that's messed up!" He was about to ask why it was this way when he was interrupted.

"Remember, your thoughts are heard here as well!" revealed the mighty voice of God. "Everything will be seen; everything will be heard."

After regaining his composure, he once again returned his concentration on his life story. He was not looking forward to some of the things in his life that are yet to replay. There will be good deeds done with ill motives, and things done weakly but with a pure conscience; but for now he will have to watch and wait.

There were birthday parties, family gatherings for a huge Thanksgiving dinner, and Christmas celebrations; he can vaguely remember some of the toys that the screen vividly displayed. Those were fun times he recalled; those were the best times.

The next scene showed Matthew helping his mother around the house with her daily chores. She was pregnant; Matthew remembered this summer very well! He remembers he was excited that he was going to be a big brother, and he didn't care if it was a brother or sister. He did secretly hope it was a brother so they could play baseball and football together, however if he were to gain a sister, he would be her protector. He would still play some games with her, but he was not playing with dolls! The conversations on the screens and his thoughts were one and the same; simultaneously confirming each other.

Twelve

This didn't seem to bother Matthew; maybe he was merely becoming comfortable with his inevitable situation, or maybe it was because it concerned Mandy. When it concerned his baby sister, he was always attentive. He never realized that he was this way from the beginning. He was witnessing video historical evidence of this fact. Matthew was thinking to himself that his Mom deserves all the credit. She was the one who reminded him that he would soon be the big brother, and that whenever Mom and Dad were not around, he would be the lone protector of this new member of the family. He would be a guardian and a teacher; he would have responsibilities in addition to his daily chores. He would lose playtime…very valuable to a six-year old kid, but he accepted his new role.

Matthew would estimate that his mother was around eight months pregnant in that last scene. It will not be long before he can see if he will continue feeling the same way about the upcoming addition to the family. Apparently, he was not paying as much attention to his life story as he thought; maybe all of his thoughts had distracted him, because he was brought back to reality when his Mom yelled.

"Matthew! Matthew, please come here, now!" Natalie shrieked. "Mathew, I need your help!"

A terrified little boy came running into the kitchen. Before she had said she needed help, he was afraid that he had done something wrong. "What's wrong, Mom?" he asked.

"Matthew, remember how we practiced our routine for the day that I had to go to the hospital?" Natalie asked. She was now experiencing some serious labor pains, and she could see that her expressions were frightening Matthew. "Don't be scared, honey! This is God's way of telling us that the baby is ready to join our family! Now, do you remember what we practiced?"

"Yes, Mom, I remember! I am to get your suitcase from the closet and you are supposed to call Dad!" Matthew exclaimed.

"Very good, honey! Go ahead and get the suitcase and set it by the front door so you can take it to the car when daddy gets here!" Natalie smiled as she gave Matthew his instructions. The pains were intense, but she could not let Matthew see how much they hurt. She called Jacob to tell him the news. "It's time, daddy! Get here as soon as you can!"

Jacob hurriedly answered as he was hanging up the phone and grabbing his car keys at the same time, "I'm on my way!"

Matthew was at the front door waiting impatiently for his Dad to arrive. He suddenly turned to go back into the kitchen for his Mom was still in there. "Can I get you anything, Mom? Do you need me to help you to the couch like Dad does sometimes? he asked.

Natalie smiled at her little man. He was doing either a great job of not being scared or an even better job at hiding it from her. "Yes, honey, you can help me!" she told him. As they walked into the living room, she looked down at Matthew and he looked as if he had achieved a monumental accomplishment. He was smiling proudly as he held on to her hand. After she collapsed into the couch, she asked, "Matthew, would you please get me a cold washcloth? Make sure you wring out as much of the water as you can before you bring it to me!"

Matthew was already halfway in the kitchen when his words finally escaped from his lips. "Yes, Mom, I'll be right back!" When he returned, he placed the cool washcloth on his Mom's forehead. "Can I get you anything else, Mom?" he asked.

"I'm okay now; thanks, Matthew! I'm sure glad you are here! You are a big help to me! Now go watch for daddy! He should be here any second!" Natalie replied.

Jacob pulled into the drive just as Matthew was arriving at the front door. Just as they had practiced, Matthew grabbed the suitcase and carried it out to the car. Jacob winked at him as they ran past each other. He set the suitcase in the middle of the backseat, and he sat down by the window and watched as his Dad carried Mom to the car, then gently sat her down in the front passenger seat, fastened her seatbelt, and closed her door. And as fast as you can say epidural, they were on their way.

The wait at the hospital seemed like days to little Matthew. However, it was several hours since he last seen his Mom. His Dad was with Mom, too, so he just had his comic books and the maternity floor supervisor/nurse to help occupy his time. She was always reassuring him that everything was okay.

Finally, his Dad came out of the area where he and Mom were. "You have a baby sister, Matthew!" Jacob exclaimed. "I'll be back in a minute and take you to meet her!"

Matthew could not remember much of the events that he was witnessing before his eyes. However, he can vaguely recall meeting his sister for the first time. She was red and wrinkly and she didn't have very much hair. He remembered thinking that she was going to need his protection! He was going to have his work cut out for him!

He got to ride up front with his Dad on the trip home. He wasn't paying attention to the conversation; he was looking at the smile on his Dad's face. He was practically oozing with pride and happiness. He noticed a smile on his face, as well. He loved alone time with his Dad. Now he begins to rummage through the files of his memory to try to isolate the time in his life when it all began to change. He realizes it is his fault alone. At this point, he feels as if all the things that went wrong in his life were his fault. Matthew sighed, lowered his head, and closed his eyes in bitter disappointment. He is only through six years of the review of his life, and despite the happy and even joyous moments, he feels a deep regret and sadness.

When he lifted his head and once again focused his attention on his life story playing before him, his sister, Mandy, was now at home. In this scene, Matthew estimated that she was probably six to eight months old. She was crawling everywhere in the house, and he was attempting to capture her attention by making silly faces. This worked for a brief moment; and after a few giggles, she was bored, and began crawling exuberantly through the living room and into the kitchen. It seemed as if all his days this particular summer was tending to his baby sister. This may explain the bond that is between them, Matthew thought to himself.

Matthew only half-heartedly paid attention to the scenes over the next few years of his life. When a scene from his school days appeared on the screens, he became startlingly alert. It was from when he was in the fifth grade; he remembers the events very well. It had started out as an ordinary spring day at Central School; our pledge of allegiance, English, math, recess, spelling, gym, and finally it was lunch. When lunch was over, it was supposed to be social studies; however, today was different... very different, indeed.

Matthew knew he was not one of the most athletic, strongest, or best-looking boys in his class. He was, however, one of the smartest, and that did not make many friends, as geeks or nerds were not necessary for any of the "cool" activities. This perceived lack of physical skills caused him to avoid conflict; he feared for his survival if he were ever in a fight. This made the events that are now replaying even more astonishing to him.

His teacher, Mrs. Williams, had called him outside the classroom before returning to his seat following lunch hour. "Matthew, we have a problem. Is there anything you would like to tell me about what happened on the playground after you finished your lunch?"

"I don't know, Mrs. Williams. I just tossed the football with some of the guys," Matthew answered. "We dropped one of the passes and it bounced against a window, but it didn't break! Did we do something wrong?"

Mrs. Williams explained, "Did you get in a fight with Henry Holt? Jenny Fisher said you busted his nose and scraped him up pretty good! Do you have anything to say for yourself?"

Matthew answered, "You're kidding me, right? I beat up Henry Holt? Mrs. Williams, you know what goes on in the school. Over the years that I have been coming here, have you ever heard of me being in a fight?"

"Well, no, but this is now! Can you explain this?" Mrs. Williams asked.

"I don't know what to say! I know that Henry is a real tough guy! He always wins his fights, and he has been in a few! How could someone like me have a chance against someone like him? He would pulverize me! Anyway, he is Jenny's boyfriend, and Henry hates me! Maybe he told Jenny to blame me to see me get in trouble! I mean, if I was in a fight with him, would I have walked away without any damage to me? I mean, look at me! Do I look like I was in a fight? If I had beat Henry up, it would have been all over the playground; heck, it would probably be all over the school! Has anyone else said that I did it?" Matthew swiftly questioned. "Has anybody else said that I beat him up?"

"No, they haven't," Mrs. Williams answered. "Jenny said that you attacked him behind the gym."

"On the baseball field? They were playing softball back there! Somebody had to see this fight! I was passing football on the other end of the playground! I told you that already!" Matthew protested. "Remember the pass that hit the window? Ask them! Ask Danny, Tim, and Jimmy! They will tell you that I was playing football!"

"Well, we'll let the principal question everyone, and I will tell him to talk to the boys you said were playing football. You can go on back in to class, but you are not to talk to anyone! You definitely cannot talk to any of the boys that you said were playing football with you! Do you understand, Matthew?" Mrs. Williams asked.

"Yes, Mrs. Williams", Matthew answered solemnly.

The rest of the afternoon moved at a snail's pace. He was quiet, just as he was supposed to be, but every time the principal called from his classroom, he would get nervous; and when they returned, they were not quiet. They would whisper to the person in front and back of them, and then the stares shifted towards him. It made matters worse.

Finally, they called Matthew's name. It was his turn to go to the office. As he walked to the office, he wondered what the principal learned from all the questioning. He wondered if he should walk or run to the office. He did not want to seem too eager and he did not want to seem guilty. How much time is enough time? He ran the stairs, skipping a step with each jump, and then walked briskly the rest of the way. He knew he did not do anything, so he shouldn't worry. His friends would tell the same story he told Mrs. Williams; he was playing football. He walked into the office and sat down in a chair by the secretary's desk. "What a way to end the day", he thought to himself.

"Matthew, come on in", the principal, Mr. Stevenson announced. Mr. Stevenson was a big man; he was over six feet tall, with broad shoulders and huge muscles. And rumor has it his heart is big, as well. He had a reputation for being fair; however, if you willfully or deliberately broke the rules, the punishment will be swift, and it will be severe. "Let's see if we can settle this before the bell rings. It's been quite a day, wouldn't you say, young man?"

Matthew stood up and followed Mr. Stevenson into his office. "Yes, sir, it has been", he answered as he stopped and stood in front of the desk. "It has been one of the longest days of my life!"

Mr. Stevenson smiled, "Well sit down, Matthew. Let's hurry and get this over with, what do you say? I'm sure you are ready to go home, aren't you?"

"You have no idea!" Matthew quickly replied.

"Well, let's get right to it! Matthew, why is it that you and Henry do not get along?" Mr. Stevenson asked.

"I don't know, sir. I try to get along with everyone, but if someone is mean or just a plain bully, I just try to avoid him or her. It's safer that way." Matthew answered.

"How or why did it escalate to this point? What about Jenny; do you get along with her?" Mr. Stevenson continued with his questioning.

"Well, she lives about a mile and a half from me. We play softball together sometimes. I mean, with some of the other kids that live near us, not just the two of us!" Matthew answered, stumbling through the question. "I guess we get along okay. We have never had any arguments or anything."

Before I tell you what I have concluded, is there anything you would like to say or add to what you told Mrs. Williams? Now is the time to do so", Mr. Stevenson permitted.

Matthew gazed down at the floor for a moment before answering, "No, sir, I don't. I told Mrs. Williams everything that I know! I can't answer about something I know nothing about, and I have no idea what happened to Henry."

Mr. Stevenson walked around his desk and sit down in the chair next to Matthew. "Matthew, you are an excellent student; you have always made excellent grades. I have never had you in this office for anything other than when you would bring papers to me from your teachers. You always seem to be in good spirits. You seem to try to get along with everyone; you do not pick on the younger kids. They like you, too. That is why this completely floored me! I was disappointed to hear that you were involved in an incident of fighting"-

"But Mr. Stevenson, sir, I was not in a fight!" Matthew interrupted.

Mr. Stevenson continued, "Matthew, let me finish!"

"I'm sorry, sir." Matthew apologized.

"Now, as I was saying, I was disappointed to hear that you were involved in a fight. That does not mean that I believed it. An accusation is just that. And until there is proof of the accusation, there is no foundation to establish punishment. Do you understand what I am saying, Matthew?" Mr. Stevenson asked.

"Yes, sir, I think so. Are you saying that I am innocent until you have proof that I am guilty?" Matthew replied.

Mr. Stevenson laughed, "Well, that is a little extreme, but, yeah, that is what I am saying. Anyway, I have talked to all of the boys that you said were playing football, and I have talked to some of the kids that were playing in the softball game that you mentioned you noticed while you were playing. Your friends did say that you were all playing football; however, you were the only one that mentioned the football hitting the window! That was a very honest thing to do, Matthew. No one from the softball field could remember seeing you anywhere near the field; however, there was one person that remembered seeing Jenny and Henry by the fence next to the swimming pool. It appears that no one was paying much attention to them, or remembers anyone else being around them the entire time they were back there. We confronted Jenny and Henry with the information we had discovered and asked if either of them would like to change anything about their story. Jenny recanted and said that it wasn't you; Henry had let Jenny hit him and they were going to blame you because Henry was sick of your good guy image. He wanted to make you look bad. So, Matthew, I apologize that all of this happened; please understand we have to take all accusations seriously, no matter who is involved. And one more thing, if Jenny is a neighbor, and she is trying to hurt you as well, you may want to let her team win the softball game occasionally! Do you like Jenny?

"I thought I did! I'm not too sure now!" Matthew softly answered; he was dejected that Jenny would have tried to hurt him.

"Maybe you're not paying enough attention to her! Girls can do crazy things when they don't get the attention they want!" Mr. Stevenson quipped.

Matthew just smiled politely at Mr. Stevenson. "Yes, sir; so, does this mean that I'm in the clear? Did you tell Mrs. Williams that I did not do it?"

Mr. Stevenson replied, "Yes, you are cleared; and I will tell Mrs. Williams after school is dismissed. You can go back to class now, Matthew, for the last ten minutes of your school day. You know, Mrs. Williams told me your response when she confronted you with the accusation. That sounded like a lawyer talking. You handled yourself very maturely for your age! You should be proud of yourself!"

Matthew beamed, "Thank you, sir!"

Matthew smiled as he watched this part of his life replayed before him. This was the point that he decided he was going to become an attorney. Matthew thought, "It's really wild how an event in your life can have such a profound effect on your entire future!"

Thirteen

"Yes, it is, isn't it, Matthew?" replied the thunderous voice that had been silent for a very long time.

The response to his thoughts surprised Matthew. He had temporarily forgotten where he was and that his thoughts are audible as well. He was thinking about the comment Mr. Stevenson made. I saw Jenny every day. I always spoke to her. We always seemed to have fun playing together. But it seemed she always had a boyfriend. She never seemed, to him anyway, to show any interest in him that way.

The review of the next two years of Matthew's life was routine. There were family vacations, birthday parties, holidays; you know… typical family activities. There were the walks with Mandy along the old railroad tracks. It was when they had their long talks; the ones where she could ask some very profound questions. She didn't seem to see the world the way society sees it. Oh, there were also the pillow fights, the mud baths, and even one of the rare arguments they had. All of this history brought Matthew several smiles, a few episodes of laughter, and a few segments of tears. The times of anger, the times he wasn't more respectful to his parents, and the times he ignored his sister. She told him things she wouldn't tell their parents. She looked up to him; as a kid he kind of liked it, but as an adult he could not for the life of him understand why she valued and respected his insight and opinion all of those years.

Matthew was so lost in his thoughts that he didn't realize that he was at Jenny Fisher's house. Another one of the many summer softball games that occur every year was taking place. Everyone that usually plays was there...except for Jenny. She was enjoying the air-conditioned comfort of her family's new home. Maybe she was the smart one!

It was the summer of his thirteenth birthday; he was now officially a teenager! Funny thing is he didn't feel any different. He had heard many stories from the kids in school about the many things to look forward to since you are no longer a child. It was the beginning of what he had hoped would be a summer of great adventures.

The game went rather quickly; however, everyone wanted to play another game. Everyone walked over to Jenny's house to sit on the porch of this beautiful new home. Since all of the other players lived anywhere from 100 yards to two-tenths of a mile away, everyone decided they would take a break to grab something cool to drink and maybe a bite to eat to re-charge their energy. By this time, Jenny had come out to see what was going on.

"What's going on? Did you all wimp out already?" Jenny asked.

Kevin, a close neighbor to Jenny, and still a kid at ten years old, replied, "No, we didn't! We're just taking a break before we play another game! Besides, you're the wimp! You ain't playin'! We're all going to go home and grab a snack and a drink and we will start back in about an hour!"

Kevin and Jenny exchanged grimaces and sticking their tongues out at each other. Jenny then politely replied, Matthew, you can stay here if you don't want to go all the way back home. I can get you a glass of iced tea or ice water if you like."

Matthew eagerly replied, "Thank you, Jenny! A glass of ice water would be great!"

"You know, since everyone is leaving, you can come inside and sit in the air conditioning while you're waiting for them to come back", Jenny offered.

"Thanks! That would be great!" Matthew readily accepted.

Everyone jumped on their bikes and rode off to their homes, and the girls from next door began walking back to their house. At the same time, Matthew was following Jenny into the front door of this absolutely beautiful and immaculate new home.

Even though she had not participated in any of the many outside activities, she was wearing a bright yellow bikini top and a pair of very bright, and very short, yellow shorts. The bikini top was very low cut and fit very well fitting. The shorts were very thin; this cotton/polyester blend allowed her to be cool but look extremely hot.

Matthew examined every inch of Jenny's beautifully tanned body. It was a natural tan…no tanning booth for her! And what Matthew could see, there were no tan lines, which intrigued him more.

As she closed the door behind the two of them, Jenny said, "I'll get you that ice water I promised you!", and then she sashayed into the kitchen. The design of the home was open, which allowed Matthew to follow every step and every move Jenny made. When she returned, he could see the obvious results of the effects of Jenny's time outside and returning to the cool comfort of her home. Jenny noticed Matthew's eyes drinking up her entire body; she smiled softly, but she also felt the tingle of achievement at the same time. "Would you like to go back and see my room?"

Matthew watched this scene from his life very intensely and very apprehensively. He could plainly see what he was thinking as a young boy. The lust was all too obvious to him, looking at his actions and mannerisms. His smile and his eyes were not helping him much, either. Jenny certainly noticed it. But he also saw something else while watching all of this; he noticed something that the naive and innocent young Matthew never saw: the lust and the anticipated excitement that was in Jenny's eyes.

"Maybe the next time", he heard himself reply as his attention returned to the screens. "I'm really not cleaned up enough to go in to your room! I mean, girls like to keep a clean room, right?"

Jenny's eyes seemed to dim slightly. Her smile, though now forced, showed her disappointment. She nodded in agreement. "Yeah, maybe next time", she answered softly.

Matthew could not believe what he had just witnessed. As he was running a gamut of emotions at the time, he was also bitterly ashamed of himself to realize that he had began his appreciation and his desire for women when he was thirteen. His shame was not from his desire, but for the lust that he had seen on his own face. "Is it still that obvious now... I mean was it still that obvious?" he wondered out loud to himself. "Are we going to show my entire life?" Matthew then immediately answered his own question, "Of course, you idiot! You get to witness the rest of your almost feeble attempt of resembling a gentleman!"

After his comments, Matthew cowered against the podium where he stood. He knew this was tame compared to what was ahead; he knew that there were worse things to come.

Much of the scenes Matthew was watching now consisted of his junior and high school years. Matthew never really had any problems with the academic portion of his education; he just seemed to be able to grasp the things as his teachers explained them. However, he did struggle with trigonometry. He loved math, so he went to the next level. Four weeks into the course, he realized this was a mistake. Other than that little glitch, his grades were excellent. He noticed that he never really spent much time studying; of course, there was always the late night cramming for a major test, but otherwise there were very few scenes of him with his nose in a book, so to speak.

"There was a reason for that", Matthew thought. There were chores to do after school; there were his neighbors that he was always helping, and once Mandy became old enough, she took some of those tasks from him. On occasion, he and his friends would go into town for a "just be boys" time of um, rest and relaxation. This was when he tried smoking; he didn't see what was so cool about it. It was the most nauseating thing he had ever tried! It was the time when he had his first drink of alcohol. First, it was beer. It wasn't bad, but it wasn't good, either. Then it was wine coolers; these were better than kool-aid. Next on the list was wine: that one could go either way, but he was going to remain neutral until he tried others. Finally, it was the harder stuff. The bourbon was too much for him; the vodka was even worse. "Man, I will never drink this stuff," He thought to himself, he didn't want the other boys to laugh at him. He was never the one that obtained the 'adult things', but he went along with the other boys and tried everything.

The next step in the growing up phase of the lives of Matthew and his friends came while they were playing Little League baseball together. One of the boys had very, uh, 'modern' parents, and he began to bring various styles of adult magazines to each game. Every game meant a different book; every book was a different format. Each book had its own diversity of women; one would go for the classy image, one would go for the seductive image, and the others were mostly just trying to be, well, lewd. All of the other boys would make comments, describing the sexual innuendos that would take place should they ever meet one of these women.

When it was time for his input, he calmly asked them, "Guys, wouldn't you like to know something about them before you started fulfilling your own personal fantasy? Besides, none of you could handle any of those women! They probably have more miles on them than our bikes do!"

This comment caused an outburst of spontaneous laughter from everyone. The boy who brought the magazines, his name Matthew could not recall, spoke up after he stopped his guffaw, "That is why we don't need to know them, bone-head! What do you think; these women want love, Mr. Romantic? It's all about the sex, man! Why else would they do this unless they were easy? Man, you've got a lot to learn, Matty boy!"

This went on until around the last two weeks of the season, when he began to bring hardcore magazines to the games. They were full of photographs of couples, sometimes three, four, and even more, engaging in various sexual activities. While all of the other boys seemed to absorb and enjoy all of the different forms of lasciviousness, Matthew yielded his attention to the one-on-one action, and focused attention more heavily on the stories. The stories explained, in detail, sexual encounters that the writer was willing to share. He also awarded an equal amount of attention to the advice column. "A few pointers," he thought to himself, "can't hurt. I may actually be able to use this someday."

Soon the baseball season was over, and our smut provider and his family moved to Alabama, so everyone seemed to forget all about the magazines; at least, nobody talked about them. It was now time to find other things to occupy their time; they needed something to do during the week to enjoy the rest of the summer before school started again. But they still had the beginning of their weekend planned for the rest of the year.

On Saturdays, every Saturday, just like clockwork, they would be among the many teens at the local theatre. Nobody seemed to care what the movie was; everyone seemed to be there for a different reason. Of course, many were actually there to watch the movie with no other agendas. The few had other reasons for being there made their agendas, their quest, be known to any that cared to listen. The presentation was different, the words varied somewhat, but the bottom line was the same: they were trying to get, or keep, a boyfriend or girlfriend before school started back. And still another small group was just looking for time alone in the dark so they could be a couple. You know; do some things that you cannot do around your parents.

Matthew has is own fond memories of the theatre that summer. It is the place he experienced his first real kiss; you remember... the one that was not a peck on the cheek or a mere smack of the lips. He cannot recall her name, or the name of a couple others.

However, he did remember the name of one young girl that he met there that summer; the one that he thought was beautiful, the one everyone else thought was just okay. Kathi Dean was her name. He saw someone special; you can call it love at first sight, but he knew there was something different about her. She seemed to brighten any room she entered. She was always smiling. He and Kathi were acquaintances more than they were friends; he never got the opportunity to get close to her; he wanted to know everything about her, but it never happened. Matthew remembered it was the biggest regret he had about being so insecure, withdrawn, and simply fearful of rejection as a teenager.

He had to re-live the death of his great-grandmother and his favorite aunt, but he also got to re-live some very special Thanksgiving and Christmas holidays with his family; he also got to enjoy his sixteenth birthday and some of Mandy's special birthday parties, as well. He vividly remembers laughing uncontrollably at her first; she dived headfirst into the cake, and emerged as an icing covered cutie, and now he was watching a simple family celebrated birthday, just Mom, Dad, him, and Mandy. Since he knew he had just turned sixteen earlier, this was her eleventh birthday. This is when his sister began asking the tough questions; the questions that were insightful beyond her age.

Fourteen

Shortly after his sixteenth birthday, Matthew had obtained a job in order to buy a car. He wanted to be one of the kids that drove to school instead of riding the bus. He wanted to be among the "cool" kids, and he did not want to go all the way home on the bus just to drive back to work. He could do his homework before he began his shift. It wasn't a glamorous job, but it allowed him to get a nice car. He worked tirelessly at the pizzeria. He was responsible for several different tasks; besides assisting in the preparation of the pizza orders, he was also a waiter, he was responsible for prepping the dough, and for washing the dishes. It wasn't all glamorous! This is where he met Pam. Pamela Murphy will be a sophomore at Duke this fall, and she has a friend that lived nearby who will be attending Duke this fall as well; both of them were Political Science majors. Pam would always stop in to eat whenever she would visit her friend She always made an effort to speak to Matthew when she came in. This helped boost his confidence somewhat. One Saturday afternoon, it was slower than normal, and Matthew was bored; he still had four hours left on his shift, and since the owner was modestly well off and didn't want to work hard if he didn't have to, he was being paid to be there just in case the circumstances changed. He was wiping off the corner table where the last guests have just finished off a bucket of wings and a large, deep-dish, double cheese, and double meat pizza; and to wash it all down, they had two pitchers of Pepsi ® and two pitchers of Bud Light ®. It seemed impossible for two guys to eat and drink so much! When he turned around to take the dishes back to wash, he met Pam and her friend as they were coming in.

"Hey, Matt, how ya doin'?" Pam asked. She always greeted him the same way.

"Hi, Pam! I'm good! It's been slow for a Saturday!" Matthew smiled as he answered. "But I'm not complaining! We all deserve an easy day once in a while, right?"

Pam smiled back in agreement. "That's exactly right! Everybody needs to relax and enjoy life once in a while!"

"Well, I don't know if I can sit back and relax, but I don't have to work my butt of, you know what I mean?" Matthew jokingly replied.

Pam smiled brazenly and replied, "And a real nice butt, too, don't ya think, Becky?"

Becky smiled alluringly and nodded in agreement.

Matthew felt his face begin to flush. "What can I get for you lovely ladies, today?" he asked, trying to change the subject.

"We'll start with two Pepsis, please, Matt!" Pam responded as they sat down at the counter instead of a table. "We might need a minute!"

Matthew felt their eyes on him as he turned to get their drinks. He heard them laughing softly; he felt a sense of confidence begin to stir in him. His self-esteem was no longer dormant. As he filled their glasses, he turned slightly to see if he could steal a glimpse of their activity. Becky was talking into Pam's ear, as Pam's focus seemed to be on Matthew. This excited him; it made him nervous, too.

"Here you go! Two cold drinks for two hot ladies!" Matthew heard himself say. "Let me know when you are ready to order!" He had to get away before his embarrassment showed. He had never said anything like that before! He had scarcely regained his composure when he heard Pam announce they were ready. He walked back to the area they were sitting at the counter and prepared to fill their request.

"What can I get for you, ladies?" Matthew asked.

Pam requested, "We will have a small pizza with sausage, mushrooms, and pepperoni, please! Oh, and bring us some of those apple-cinnamon twists for dessert...with some extra icing!"

"Just one order of the twists?" Matthew asked.

"Of course!" Pam explained, "We should stop at the pizza; we need to keep our bodies in great shape, but they're just so good! So we're gonna be bad!"

"Even great bodies are entitled to enjoy something simply for their own satisfaction once in a while, aren't they?" Matthew inquired encouragingly. "Besides, you both have great bodies! I'm sure sharing an order and a small pizza will not cause any damage!"

"Why, thank you, Matt!" Pam replied appreciatively. "I never knew you even noticed!"

Matthew smiled uneasily, his nervousness obviously showing. "I'll bring your pizza out as soon as it's ready!" He then turned to walk into the prep station to begin making their pizza.

Matthew was noticeably uncomfortable reliving this part of his life. He had many great memories of the time working in the pizza shop, but he also knows many of the seemingly good memories are also sins against him, which he has yet to relive. He closed his eyes tightly as he ran his hands through his hair as he exhaled a deep sigh. The silence was deafening. Although he had the sounds from the people and places from the screens, but there no other people around him to allow him to share a conversation. He was isolated, but definitely not alone.

He wanted to watch; he desperately wanted to relive some of the upcoming events that made him feel more confident about himself; he was confident in his intellectual abilities, but he was now beginning to open up and not be hesitant to talk to the girls. He remembered many of the older girls would enjoy talking to him as much as he enjoyed their conversation. It made it easier to start his seemingly harmless flirtation with some of the girls as they came in the pizzeria.

Once he regained his composure, once he regained his concentration, he again lifted his eyes to the screens. Once again, he was talking to Pam. They were outside the pizzeria; Matthew remembers this day vividly. It was two weeks after an uneventful seventeenth birthday. It was a warm summer evening; a slight breeze blowing to make it perfect. He had a short shift today, and it was early enough to allow him to enjoy the evening. Pam had come in for our "just for me pizza" and the irresistible apple cinnamon twists, and she was about to finish at the same time he had finished washing off and freeing himself of any reminders of the workday. As he was walking out, he almost didn't see her sitting in the corner booth in the back. He smiled and waved. "Hello, Pam!" he called out cheerfully.

"Hello, Matt!" she enthusiastically replied. "Hey, you gotta minute? You can join me, if you like!"

Matthew had nowhere to go and nothing to do; he was going home to surf the internet and listen to some music. He nodded approvingly and walked back to her booth. "Thanks for inviting me! I hope your dinner was great! I should have known you were here when I saw the pepperoni-sausage-mushroom pizza and the twists combination!" Matthew noticed a difference in Pam this evening. See seemed more relaxed than he can recall ever seeing her; there was a special softness in her eyes and in her smile.

He also couldn't help noticing the clothes she was wearing. Her tank top was a lightly colored pink, and her shorts were white with a coordinating pink and pastel blue cross-piping design that overlaid the white; this made her beautiful tan look even darker. "So, what are you doing way over here? I thought Becky was away with her family on vacation!"

"Can't a girl get a craving?" Pam asked, smiling warmly. "I just had to have some of the food from here! It's not really that far! Besides, did you ever have a day when you really wanted something? You know; when you want something so much that nothing else would satisfy your hunger?"

Matthew assumed her reply was in response to his question; however, her eyes seemed to be thinking about something else. "Yes, I have. I know exactly what you're saying." he answered. "It was the twists, wasn't it?"

Pam didn't answer. She simply looked tenderly at Matthew and smiled. "What are you doing tonight, Matt?"

"Nothing special. Why? Do you need my help with something?" Matthew voluntarily asked.

"Would you care to hang out with me this evening? I'll understand if you say no. It's just that you act more mature than most high school seniors do! Who am I kidding? You are more mature than most of the college sophomores!" Pam confessed. "I miss Becky a little bit, and none of our friends are taking any summer classes at Duke, so I'm kind of bummed a little bit. But please, don't take it that you are the last resort! I'm sorry, I really didn't mean for it to come out like that! It sounded bad, didn't it?"

Matthew smiled reassuringly. "It's okay. I know what you meant. Actually, I'm flattered and a little embarrassed! I mean you are a beautiful college girl! I'm still in high school;

I'm not even a part of the 'in' crowd. I just want to graduate and get started on my college career."

Pam looked bowled over by Matthew's comments. "You should give yourself some credit! You are a really cool guy! You do not need to be a part of the so-called 'in' crowd! You are a very good-looking guy, too! Your girlfriend is a lucky young lady!"

Matthew felt his face flush. "There is no girlfriend." He mumbled.

Pam shook her head in amazement. "You're kidding, right? Seriously, you're not dating anyone?"

Matthew felt embarrassed. "I'm not very good with girls. There are several that I would have liked to ask out, but I didn't. I am just a little shy; I'm also not good at rejection, I mean I don't go psycho or angry; I just get depressed. My self-esteem gets a little flat", he admitted.

Pam was dumbfounded. "You're shy? Well, please explain why you can talk so easily with Becky and me! Oh, I get it. We are not anything to get nervous about, is that it?"

"No, that's not it at all!" Matthew snapped. "It's just that, first, I know that with you being college girls; second, I am a high-school senior; third, I know that I have no chance with either of you, so there is no pressure; and fourth, Becky has brought her boyfriend in here a time or two, so I know she's not on the market.

"God, Matt, you sound like a friggin' lawyer!" Pam moaned. "Tell the truth! You just talk to us because it's part of your job! You probably don't even think we are pretty!"

"Stop it! Stop it right now!" Matthew demanded. "How many times have I given the two of you compliments when you are here? Look, I'll admit, and I'm sorry, I know she's your friend, but Becky's okay, I mean she's pretty, kind of, but"-

"Hey, that's my friend you're talking about!" Pam interrupted.

"As I was saying before I was so rudely interrupted, she's okay, but it would have been even ruder of me to say you are a total babe and she's 'cute', so I was diplomatic and bestowed the same compliment to you both!" Matthew enlightened. I couldn't bear to hurt her feelings or anything; she is such a nice girl! But you already know that since she is your best friend!"

"You want to go for a ride?" Pam asked.

Fifteen

M atthew eagerly accepted. "Sure, give me a minute to organize my car a little bit; I haven't cleaned it for a couple weeks, so"-

Pam interrupted, "No, let's take my car, if that's okay!"

Matthew smiled and assured her, "That would be great!" He loved her car. It was a 1990 Volkswagen Corrado. It was bright red in color, and had a white leather interior. The car was just like her-neat, sophisticated, fast…and hot! You could not tell by looking at it that it was an older car. As they walked to the car, He asked, "Anywhere in particular we're going?"

Pam asked, "Does it matter?"

"Not really," Matthew replied. "Wherever you want to go is fine! I'm just going to enjoy my ride and my time with you!

It will be great to be out with a beautiful woman; and a college girl, too! That's like extra icing on the cake! Or, maybe I should say extra icing on the twists!"

Pam grabbed Matthew's hand to stop him for a moment. She then turned him towards her, and delicately kissed his unsuspecting lips. "Thank you, Matt; you are great for my ego! And thanks for going out with me!"

Matthew could see his reflection in her beautiful brown eyes. He could see the surprise and excitement on his face. "And you are great for mine!" Matthew softly confessed. He continued to hold her hand as he walked to the driver's side of the car; he opened her door and let go of her hand as she sat in her seat.

"And you're a gentleman, too! Are all of the girls in high school blind, or are they stupid? What ease will I find out about you tonight?" Pam asked in breathless anticipation.

"I don't know. You already know a lot about me. You know, you are in here eating quite often! You always seem to learn something about me each time," Matthew answered. "I'm hoping to learn more about you tonight, that is, if you want to tell me! I know less about you than you know about me! He closed her door and ran around to the other side of the car. He slid into the passenger seat, fastened his seat belt, and sunk back into the soft, leather seat. He closed his eye for a brief moment to try to let this entire chain of events sink in. Then he turned to look at Pam, still smiling, and said, "Let's get this night started!"

Matthew watched this part of his life history with more intensity than any other time since this evidentiary review began. He remembers this particular evening vividly. He had recalled this night several times with tender, appreciative fondness. He was smiling as a tear escaped from his eye. He blinked his eyes rapidly several times to allow the remaining tears to follow their predecessor, and again intently focused his attention to the movie that was his life.

Pam pulled out of the parking area of the pizzeria, and pulled out onto the highway. She was very adept at handling this 5-speed machine. Matthew knew of very few people that could proficiently drive a vehicle with a standard transmission, much less any females. Definitely, she was unique; she was prepared from a different pattern!

The wind was blowing her blond hair, and this allowed Matthew to enjoy seeing her neck and shoulders. This particular pair of shorts she was wearing allowed him to see the definition in her leg muscles each time she would shift gears. None of the girls in New Hope can compare to her. Sure, there are some lovely girls in New Hope, but none, in his humble observation, can compare, when you look at the total package; brains, beauty, and compassion. That makes for a very attractive combination. And he was spending the evening with her. She had asked him to go out with her! How did he get so lucky? Why was he so fortunate? Was it a case of 'right place, right time'? He didn't care. He was going to drink every moment of this evening; he was going to allow himself to become intoxicated with the events they will enjoy together, as he deduced in his finite mind that he might never have an opportunity such as this again.

"Hey, you're awfully quiet over there, Matt! What's wrong? Are you not having fun?" Pam asked curiously. She had filched a glimpse of his stares from the corner of her eye on two different occasions while she was driving.

"I'm sorry, Pam! I'm still trying to figure out how I got so lucky!" Matthew professed.

"You know, I'm not going anywhere; you can look at the sights while we're talking and driving!" Pam informed.

"Yeah, but I would rather look at the scenery in the car!" Matthew emphasized.

Pam smiled appreciatively; then she looked serious. Her countenance seemed to change almost instantly. "Matt, you always seem so interested in what I may have to say at the pizzeria. Why is that? I can't be that interesting. My vast array of conversations can even be boring to Becky!"

"Well, since you are driving and I don't particularly want to walk home, I guess 'no comment' will not suffice?" Matthew asked.

"Nope, sorry; you're out of luck! Let's have it! And it better be the truth, or you will face the consequences!" Pam revealed.

"Okay, you're holding all the cards now!" Mathew took a deep breath and exhaled forcefully before he continued. "Here goes; the truth of the matter is this... and I'm not bragging on myself, please believe me, but to explain, I need to say it. I'm sort of smart, I guess, and I guess that is another strike against me when it comes to the girls at school. I'm not a jock; I do play sports, but it's not my main priority. My education is my future. I find your conversations at times stimulating; some of the many discussions you and Becky had the last two semesters of college were an insight into what I had to look forward to when I go to college next fall."

"So, you were just using us? You were merely trying to gain insight into some college courses?" Pam questioned.

"No, wait a minute; you don't really believe that, do you? I have told you on more than one occasion that I like having a beautiful lady in the dining room! It makes my workday much more worthwhile; it makes it bearable. However, I did find fault with your theory on your ethics course thesis."

"What are you talking about? I got an 'A' in that course due to my thesis! What was wrong with it?" Pam challenged.

Matthew laughed, "I'm sorry! I love it when you become animated! You become even more alive! You are total energy!"

"Aaaarrgh! Humph! Pam shrilled. "That's just mean, Matt!" she moaned in exasperation, as she playfully punched Matthew in his shoulder. Her frustration quickly evaporated, as she reached over to rub his shoulder; she smiled tenderly and softly asked, "Do you forgive me?"

"Yeah, it's my fault, you know; I was the one that triggered your actions" Matthew informed her.

"Can you stop sounding like a damn lawyer for just a little bit? I swear Matt, is that going to be your career plan? Are you going to be the best lawyer in the world someday?" Pam asked despondently.

Matthew thought briefly before he answered. "Yes, I believe I am! I may need to save you from abuse charges or jail time someday! Hey, remember, I told you I'm not good at this girl conversation thing!"

Pam pulled as far off to the side of the gravel road as she could without going into the drainage ditch; she stopped the car, shifted the car into neutral, and set the emergency brake. "Okay Matt, quit trying so hard! Starting now, and for the rest of the evening, I just want you to be yourself, okay? Just forget that I'm a college student; forget that I'm a girl"-

"You're not asking for much, are you?" Matthew interrupted. "I suppose I am supposed to forget that you are breathtakingly beautiful, as well?" Matthew interjected.

Pam unlatched her seatbelt and leaned over towards Matthew. She put one hand on each side of his face and turned his head towards her. She shook her head in wonderment; she then leaned into his face and pressed her lips into his; she allowed them to linger there for seconds. It was not like their first kiss; this kiss was not delicate, neither was it fervent, she wanted to insure he received the message. "How can such a mature young man be inside this teenage body?" she asked amazingly. "Do we have a deal; can you be the guy back at the pizzeria and forget about what it is that may be confusing or causing the doubt and insecurity your mind? I would not be with you if I didn't want to be!"

Matthew watched himself in disbelief as he relived his stumbling and fumbling through this evening in his past. He can scarcely believe that it was as precarious as it appears; he does not remember it being this awkward, at least not yet.

"Matt, do we have a deal?" Pam asked again, causing Matthew once again to become attentive to the screens.

"Yes...I'll try my best. Just...please, be patient with me. I'll do better as the night goes on!" Matthew promised.

Pam smiled that warm, affectionate smile that had drawn him to her when she first walked into the pizzeria and into his life last year. She fastened her seatbelt, released the emergency brake, shifted the Corrado into first gear, and they were on their way. "Hey, have you ever had a sunset picnic up at The Point?"

Matthew answered naively, "Where is The Point?"

Pam smiled, "You've never been to The Point? Oh, man, are you in for a surprise...and an inspiration! It's the place you can see nearly everything in the village; but there is another view on the other side that is all nature; it's just trees, mountains, hills...nothing but nature's natural beauty! It's a great place to relax, to regain your focus, to study in peace and quiet, and to, uh, enjoy other things, too!"

"It sounds great! But wait! We don't have anything to have a picnic!" Matthew informed her.

"That's easy to fix! We'll stop at the store at the end of the road, grab us some things to eat, something to drink, and we are on our way! I've got a blanket in the back of the car, and I think I may even have a sleeping bag back there that we can use for a giant pillow, since those little red pillows in the back are more for show than comfort, you know!" Pam enlightened him with a renewed enthusiasm. "What shall we get to take with us on our picnic?"

"Please, no pizza!" Matthew pleaded.

"Don't worry, I agree; let's get some cheese and crackers, a couple of turkey subs, potato chips, maybe some grapes, no strawberries! And our beverages, of course; how does that sound?"

"It sounds good to me; what are we going to have to drink?" Matthew asked.

"Well, even though I could get us a bottle of wine or champagne, I will not drink and drive! And I do not want to risk getting caught giving it to you! How about we get a bottle of sparkling grape juice, some bottled water, and some Pepsi and we have everything covered! Is that cool?" Pam asked. "Is there anything you would like instead?"

"It sounds as if you've thought of everything, as usual!" Matthew responded heartily. "I'll just enjoy all of the new sights and experiences you have planned for me this evening!"

After their stop at the store, they began their trip up the road that leads to The Point. It is at the top of a very large hill that Matthew had passed probably thousands of times in his life, yet he has never ventured onto this particular road. As they continued up the winding and narrow road, he could not believe the beauty; it was just another old country road, but aesthetically perfect. Adorned with honeysuckle and wild roses, the aroma that filled the air was almost intoxicating. There were also blackberry bushes and wildflowers as well, which made this probably one of the most picturesque sceneries that hardly anyone knows about; at least, nobody talks about, anyway. Matthew felt somewhat cheated, having denied himself the enjoyment of all of this beauty all these years.

When Pam had reached their destination, she parked her car on the side revealing nature's beauty. She ran around to the back of the car and opened the trunk. Matthew joined her at the back of her car to help her unload all of the things they will need to enjoy this picnic. She handed him the food and beverages; she clutched the blanket under her arm and grabbed the tightly rolled sleeping bag with her free hand, and slid the strap over her shoulder to allow her to close the trunk. Matthew was waiting for Pam to direct him to the area to allow him to begin setup of their scenic dinner date.

"Follow me," Pam directed. "The perfect spot is just over by that cluster of trees. It's got the best view; watching a sunset from there is an uplifting experience the first time you witness it! Oh, Matt, it's such an awesome sight! Once you've seen one, you never get enough of them! This is my favorite place to come to study; Becky never understood why. I guess she is not as appreciative of the beauty of this world God created for us, huh?"

"Sunset, huh?" Matthew questioned. "Do you think we will be done with all of this food by then?"

Pam responded with a tranquil and calming laugh. "You never know; we may need a snack later!"

Sixteen

They began to spread the blanket out at the spot that Pam had already determined. Matthew followed by placing the food elegantly upon the blanket.

"I guess my job came in handy, after all!" Matthew declared.

"It looks great, Matt! I guess it did, indeed!" Pam announced.

When they sat down to begin, the sun had already sank to the point where it seemingly was touching the tip of the highest point of the largest mountain. The sky was beginning to fill with the colors of days' end, as the red brilliance slowly engulfed the golden radiance that once dominated. They finished with their appetizers and their sandwiches around the time as the red colors of sunset began to surrender to the purple blanket of night that was beginning to cover the sky. They shared the strawberries as they appreciated the beauty of the splendor that was constantly changing before their eyes. As they were down to the last strawberry, Pam seized it as Matthew was reaching for it.

"Hey, that's not fair!" Matthew quibbled. "You saw me reaching for it!"

Pam smiled, "Maybe next time you will be a little quicker!" As she slowly raised the strawberry to her mouth, she was carefully studying Matthew's reaction as well. "Okay, I'll share it with you!" She put half of the strawberry in her mouth, leaving the other half protruding from her lips. "If you want the other half, you need to come and take it!" Pam mumbled.

Matthew rolled over to where Pam was relaxing, supporting her position by using her elbows. As he leaned in to take the other half of the strawberry, Pam let her elbows purposely subside slowly to allow her to lie down completely as he continued to advance closer to her waiting lips. As he continued to lean closer to her, he realized he could no longer support himself at that angle, and he come to rest upon her very warm and very soft body.

After he finally took the strawberry, she began to kiss his lips tenderly and the area around his mouth, allowing him to swallow the last of their desert. When finished, it was a synchronized meeting of their lips; the kisses became longer, deeper, more passionate. He wanted to wrap his arms around her and hold her as tightly as he could; however, he was now using his elbows to support his weight to prevent all his weight from being upon Pam.

Pam, however, had her arms free now. She was using them to her advantage, too. She began by running her fingers through his hair, following that with a gentle scalp massage. She continued her journey southward as she briefly rubbed his neck; then she proceeded on to his shoulders, finally reaching his back. She allowed herself the liberty to roam freely there for a while until she felt the need to continue her exploration.

When her hands each had found their destination, Matthew could no longer contain himself. With her arms now stretched to their limit, it gave him the opening he needed. He swiftly slid his arms under her back hugged her

closely as he rolled her on top of him to allow him to recip-
rocate the favor. He thought he heard her moan softly as he
rubbed her neck. As he permitted his hands to massage her
back, he discovered that when he had rolled her on top of
him, her shirt had inadvertently slid upward, exposing the
lower part of her back. When his hands touched her bare
skin, a delicate sigh escaped from her; her kisses became
more fervent, more passionate. When they stopped to catch
their breath, they raised up to a kneeling position on their
knees. Immediately their eyes met; they saw confirmation in
what was already evident with their bodies.

Meanwhile, Matthew was watching one of the most
exciting and terrifying times in his life unfold before him.
He found himself thinking that she is still one of the most
beautiful women he has ever seen. He was surreptitiously
looking forward to reliving this time of his life; he was
shamelessly eager to see her body one more time. As his
eyes stared intensely at the screen, he realized his wish was
just moments away.

"Pam, I uh, I've never, I mean, I've never made love to
a woman yet." Matthew confessed. "I'm sorry. You can take
me back to my car now, if you want."

Pam smiled warmly. Her countenance showed her amazement of his confession. She held his hands as she asked, "Do
you want to make love to me?"

Matthew nodded approvingly and softly whispered,
"More than anything else I've ever wanted in my life. I just
don't want to disappoint"-

"Stop right there!" Pam interrupted. "I want you, Matt;
you have always made me feel good about myself when I
was feeling down, and when I was feeling good, you made
me feel great! That is something every woman desires; they
need to feel wanted, desired, loved. When you look at me
when I come in the pizzeria, I feel like the most beautiful
woman around"-

"That's because you are!" Matthew interrupted her.

Pam looked at him affectionately and asked, "How do you do it?"

"How do I do what?" Matthew asked curiously.

"Say the things you do and look like you really mean it! You are going to be a great lawyer, Matt. You are very"-

Matthew interrupted her again, "I do mean it! That is why it looks as if I do! I don't know any other way; I've always been honest, painfully at times, I must say."

"Oh, come here!" Pam ordered. She wrapped her arms around him and kissed him with a passion he had never experienced before. He knew this was the beginning of a pivotal change in his life. She encouraged him to remove her clothes; she then enthusiastically removed his. "I want to show you how much I appreciate how you've made me feel over this past, how long has it been now since we first met, a year and a half? Your compliments, encouragement, your lustful and wanting me looks, you have given me and shown me much more than my so-called ex-boyfriends ever did!" she admitted.

As she lied back on the blanket, the light of the moon allowed him to admire all of her body; he drank in all of her beauty, his eyes roaming from her head to her feet, and then returning to his original starting point. It seemed to her as if his eyes did this several times; this adoration caused her to shiver with great anticipation.

Matthew thought to himself, "I swear, she is more beautiful than anything I ever saw in those magazines!"

As Matthew continued to watch the screens with great intensity, he laughed aloud. He remembered thinking that. Only now, it was audible. That was kind of disconcerting. He thought he had heard his thoughts several times earlier, but he was unsure. He had a habit of thinking out loud, but he could not remember without doubt on the other occasions. This one he remembers clearly! There was no way anyone else knew about it! At least, he thought no one else, until now.

As Matthew and Pam shared, explored, and enjoyed each other in several different ways, the night seemed to be passing rapidly. Matthew had successfully administered Pam pleasures she had never before experienced, while everything Pam shared with Matthew was a new experience for him.

As they relaxed in one another's arms, they enjoyed the beauty of the moonlit sky. Matthew was thinking of how perfect this night has been; when he got out of bed this morning, he had no idea or even any thoughts of the events that just transpired. Pam was thinking that it's hard to believe that the young man beside her is so mature for his age. He seemed to put her desires ahead of his own; she wondered if it was because it was his first time, or his desire to fulfill his lover's needs. At this moment, she wasn't going to waste much time or put forth much effort to determine the answer. And she certainly couldn't tell him that he was her best! How could she break the silence, since he was obviously too nervous to say or ask anything. "Matthew, you are the most considerate and unselfish man I have ever known! You will definitely break a lot of hearts in college!" she complimented.

"I've got plenty of time to worry about college! I just want to survive my senior year of high school! But, thank you, you're good for my self-confidence!" Matthew replied. "Maybe it will be a great year, you know? You never can tell!"

Matthew held her close to his chest; he could feel the warmth of her body as well as the chill bumps that the cool breeze had triggered as it stirred the stagnant summer night. The kiss they shared was a long, soft, and tender kiss. He then kissed both of her cheeks, both eyes, and once more on the lips before they got dressed and headed back to reality.

While they were driving back to the pizzeria to take Matthew to his car, Pam noticed an obvious and oblivious smile on his face. It made her feel warm inside knowing that he enjoyed the evening as much as she did. When they arrived at the pizzeria, Matthew assured her, "I will not tell anyone about tonight, Pam. No one needs to know, anyway. This was just about us, right?"

Pam's mind was racing. Wow! How many guys could keep their mouth shut about their sexual encounters? There is no way he is this good! "Um, okay, Matt; thank you, I appreciate that! People can really trash a girl if you know what I mean!" Pam answered gratefully. "Don't you think someone will figure it out if we are hanging out all summer, I mean, if you want!"

Matthew wasn't sure, but it sounded to him like she was not going to avoid him or any awkward moments this summer. "I think we can manage! Nobody around here would believe I was hanging out with a college girl, anyway. Becky, on the other hand, might be a different story!" Matthew confided.

Pam responded, "Matthew, I think that you could make her believe whatever you wanted her to believe!"

Before he got out of the car, he leaned over to kiss her once more. "Thank you for the most memorable evening in my life! You are so beautiful, so full of passion; how did I get this lucky?"

Pam smiled. "Okay, enough of the accolades for tonight! Save some for later!" she requested. "Matt, I am going to be visiting some friends from high school this weekend, so I will not be in. I just wanted you to know so that you wouldn't think I was avoiding you," she shared. "If you see Becky before Sunday, tell her that I will call her before I leave Jana's house. You know cell reception is a bummer out here sometimes. I'll stop in when I get back. Don't get too many girlfriends while I'm gone!"

"That won't happen!" Matthew reported. "Be safe, and have fun; and you can think about me if you want!"

Pam smiled, waved goodbye, and drove away. Matthew knew he was not going to sleep much tonight.

Matthew had closed his eyes to rest for a few minutes; seventeen plus years of his life already replayed for him and he realized he was not sleepy. However, he was getting the same feeling he gets, rather he got, when he used to look over case files before a trial. He would spend hours tirelessly searching each piece of information, evidence, testimonies or whatever else may be in the file to help strengthen his case. That was usually hours, sometimes days, but this was years! This was another concern that was starting to develop within his mind.

He knew that the events of the past evening would only happen two more times during this summer; the rest of the days seemingly meant nothing to him. They were all simply routine, mundane. However, he noticed that Becky looked at him differently, or was he seeing her differently? Did Pam tell her about them? He was not going to say anything; and he definitely was not going to ask Pam if she told her! So what if she knew? Girls share their stories just like men do, don't they?

Seventeen

He paid close attention to his intimate nights with Pam. The third and the last time they were together, she revealed that this was also good-bye. She waited until their exchange of passion was complete before she told him. It was almost a poetic way of saying good-bye. A professor at Columbia read the thesis that she had written in her spring ethics class, shared them with the school's board of directors, finally with the school president, and he had obtained grants that would allow her to transfer, if she would like. She knew this was an opportunity of a lifetime; in addition, with her tuition now paid, this meant no more college debt for her and her parents! If she wanted to pursue a career in politics or in Washington, D.C., this was as good as it gets.

He relived his senior year of high school; he was a starter on the football team, but he accomplished nothing spectacular. He was captain of the debate team, again; just as he did last year, he was state champion in individual debate, and his team was state team champions for the first time. There was no steady girlfriend; there were very few dates to consider worth reliving the moments. He had cut his work schedule back to only weekends. That meant working on Sundays;

that meant during one of the most crucial times in his life, he was not receiving ammunition to fight off the enemy.

Matthew was very busy. He was submitting applications, gathering information, taking tests, and all of the things you need to do in order to organize and ease the transition into college life. He knew he wanted to be an attorney; he needed to narrow down his personal list of 'the best colleges to become a successful attorney' to three by his self-imposed deadline of January 1st.

He had done better than that; he had decided on Duke University before Christmas. He did not want to deal with it any longer or let it interfere with the Christmas break from school. He wanted to focus all of his energy on filling his mind with knowledge that would prepare him for his career. His confidence was not a question; he purposed in his mind and in his heart to become a great and successful attorney. He was not the class valedictorian, but his grades placed him in the top ten.

Summer vacation was not a vacation for Matthew. It was working 40 hours a week, helping Mandy with the chores at home and helping her with the tasks and errands that their neighbors were not able to do. Becky had introduced him to one of her new friends, Sandy. She was also an old friend of Pam. She and Becky were going to be roommates at college this fall. They had found an apartment close to the college; they wanted to be a big part of the social scene outside of their academic commitments. Why they shared this information with him was unknown to him. Becky knew he was going to Duke, but she also knew that he would probably be living at home.

Matthew noticed that Becky looked at him differently since Pam had left. She and Sandy were whispering, and by the expression on their face, he could tell they were enjoying the conversation. And when he realized their focus was on him, he knew he was the subject of their conversation. He was enjoying the attention, but he missed Pam. He did not have the time, or the desire, to get involved with someone right now. He was ready to begin the pursuit of his degree; he was ready to begin his life.

Watching the next six years of his life was, well, stimulating and distressing. While he enjoyed reliving his academic accomplishments, he did not prefer to relive the parties or the drinking benders in which he and his friends were eager participants. He especially did not care to relive any of the sexual trysts that he was involved in during those parties. While some were pleasant memories, some were regrettable and forgettable. However, right now, he is regretting all of them.

He suddenly remembered all of the things he had heard in church while growing up as a teenager; Galatians 5:19 was first- "Now the works of the flesh are evident, which are adultery, fornication, uncleanness, lewdness", then it was I Thessalonians 4:3, "For this is the will of God, your sanctification: that you should abstain from sexual immorality". The next piercing reminder came from Job 24:15, "The eye of the adulterer waits for the twilight, saying, 'no one will see me'; and he disguises his face." The next arrow came from II Timothy 2:22, "Flee also youthful lusts". The weight of his indiscretions, all of his sins, was prohibiting Matthew from standing tall and erect as he usually does. He begun to slouch; his back was now slightly bent and his shoulders were wilting.

There was one thing that was deeply troubling him; the voice that he was hearing in his head was not that of his pastor from his church. It sounded more like a softer version of the voice he was hearing thundering before him on this ordeal; he was sure he was hearing the voice of God. To complicate matters even more, he realized that he had heard that voice, or thought he had, several times over the course of his teen and college years; when it interfered with his desires, he conveniently ignored it; he blatantly disobeyed it.

"Maybe the events of this ordeal are beginning to take a toll on my mind," Matthew thought. "Maybe I no longer even have control of my mind, maybe I'm losing my mind!"

While he secretly enjoyed reliving some of the past moments, he suddenly realized that his secret enjoyment was not a secret here; this caused him embarrassment, no, it was shame he was experiencing, as well as regret. He knew there was still a lot more to see, a lot more that he has done. He was not a murderer, a child predator, an armed robber, even though some would argue this one; he respected his parents, loved his family, and cared for and helped his neighbors whenever he could. How severe will his punishment be?

Of course, as if on cue, his life was now at a Sunday morning service he had attended, at Mandy's insistence, while he was home after graduation. He had already accepted a job in New York, and his firm had furnished him with an apartment. It was nothing fancy, but it was free. He was spending a few weeks with the family before he moved to begin this exciting time in his life.

The preacher was on vacation, and it was one of the elders, Billy Dunn, scheduled to present the message on this morning. Matthew remembered him from youth class. He was an excellent teacher; he presented the message he wanted to convey without trying to condemn anyone. He always told us that whatever we may have done, he has done it or some one else in the church has; and if God forgave them, He will forgive us, too.

It was overwhelming for Matthew to watch how things, events, situations in his life were happening for a purpose; as he watched the events in his life, he could see how God had given him a means of avoiding the things that were to happen in the future. The message he was about to hear was no different.

Elder Billy began by asking, "Is there anyone here this morning that wonders or has ever wondered what it's going to be like when we stand before God? Did you ever wonder what He looked like? Ever wonder how His voice will sound? How many of you are just too busy worrying if you have messed up somewhere at sometime in your life and it has not been forgiven?" He paused to allow time for thought and reflection. "What if I told you that you are wasting your time and energy? What if I told you how you would never have to worry about anything in your life ever again?"

The whispers and mumbles were buzzing throughout the entire sanctuary. This seized Matthew's attention; he had to hear what Billy was going to say next. He wondered how, as he tried remembering everything he had been taught over the years, can it be possible to live worry free.

Billy began speaking again, "Turn in your Bibles to Matthew, chapter six. I'll try not to confuse or offend anyone, but the fact is I'm just the messenger. God said it. It was through His son, Jesus, that we become aware of how we should live worry free. Jesus gave the famous 'Sermon on the Mount' before thousands of people. The wisdom He shared with them is still true for us today. Is everyone on Matthew chapter six? Good! Now, go to verse twenty-five. It says, and this is Jesus talking, it's in red, so that means it is important, right? Okay, verse twenty-five, Jesus said, 'Therefore I say to you, do not worry about your life, what you will eat or what you will drink; nor about your body, what you will put on. Is not life more than food and the body more than clothing?' Let's continue reading. In verses twenty-six and twenty-seven Jesus says, 'Look at the birds of the air, for they neither sow nor reap nor gather into barns; yet your heavenly Father feeds them. Are you not of more value than they? Which of you by worrying can add one cubit to his stature?'

Billy stopped for a moment to share, "I remembering sharing this at some point in my life with a group, and I remember one lady getting very upset with me after I had finished speaking. She walked up to me and said, 'Brother Billy, I know that the Bible says not to worry, but I'll tell you this: I know for a fact that worrying helps!' Well I just had to ask; you know the phrase, if you ask a silly question,"-

The congregation answered in unison, "You get a silly answer!"

Billy laughed, "You got it! I asked her to provide me with her proof. She calmly but hardheartedly replied, 'Everything I ever worried about never happened! It was only when I didn't worry that things happened!' Well, I could not just let it go; I mean, she opened the door for me, who am I to be rude and not accept her invitation to walk on in? I asked her, 'Did you know about the things that happened before they happened in order to allow you the opportunity to worry about them?' She answered me, and with a straight face she said, 'No, that's kind of stupid, Billy! If I had known, I could have worried!'

Billy returned the focus to the message he was conveying to the congregation. "You laugh at that little story; but how many of you worry about things in which you have absolutely no control in the outcome or the circumstances? If you are a parent, you should be concerned for your children. Since you are a child, or were one at one time, you should be concerned about your parents, if they are still living. Let's go down to verse thirty. Jesus says, 'Now if God so clothes the grass of the field, which today is, and tomorrow is thrown into the oven, will He not much more clothe you, O you of little faith?' Now go on down to verse thirty-three, and this is still Jesus talking, He says, 'But seek first the kingdom of God and His righteousness, and all these things shall be added to you. Therefore do not worry about tomorrow, for tomorrow will worry about its own things. Sufficient for today is its own trouble'

Billy could see the questions and confusion on some of the faces. "Jesus was talking a lot about food, clothing, and shelter. But if you look in verse twenty-five, He said do not worry about your life. In verse thirty-four, He was trying to point out that we have enough going on in our life to add worry to it. None of us are guaranteed tomorrow; I'm not trying to sound morbid, but someone or everyone in this congregation this morning could die before our evening service tonight. I'm not saying we shouldn't make plans; we have to plan, we have to prioritize and organize. But God does not want us so wrapped up in worry and fear that it paralyzes us from doing the work He has called us to do!

Billy once again paused for a moment. This time, it was a little longer pause. "I still have not answered the question I asked when I started this message. The Holy Spirit wanted to go in a different direction, and it was not what I had planned. Now, I didn't worry, but I was nervous! Has the Spirit ever done that to anyone else in here?" Billy asked as he raised his hand in the air. After the congregation had lowered their hands, he continued. "Is there someone here today that wonders if their salvation is secure? Do you wonder if your prayer was heard, or if you said the right things? Well you should not worry anymore after this morning! I am going to tell you the Bible's stance on your questions, your doubts. Is the Bible true?"

The congregation replied with an assortment of, "Yes!" and "Amen" and he even heard a couple of "Come on!" in the midst.

Billy continued with his message. "Turn with me to the book of Romans, chapter ten. I'm going to start in verse one and continue through to verse thirteen. I may skip a verse or two, but I'll try to let you know ahead of time, okay? Okay, verse one, Paul was talking to the people of Israel;

but, where Paul says 'Israel', I want you to put your name in there instead! Here we go; verse one says, 'Brethren, my heart's desire and prayer to God for Israel is that they may be saved. For I bear witness that they have a zeal for God, but not according to knowledge. For they being ignorant of God's righteousness, and seeking to establish their own righteousness, have not submitted to the righteousness of God. For Christ is the end of the law for righteousness to everyone who believes.'

Billy stopped reading for a moment to add, "Paul was not necessarily saying they were trying to deem themselves righteous, although there were probably some that did, he was saying that they had not submitted to God! They had not searched the words that Christ had given them to seek the assurance that they wanted and needed! Let's go to verse eight. Verse eight says, 'But what does it say? 'The word is near you, in your mouth and in your heart' (that is, the word of faith which we preach): that if you confess with your mouth the Lord Jesus and believe in your heart that God raised Him from the dead, you will be saved. For with the heart one believes unto righteousness, and with the mouth confession is made unto salvation.'

Billy added more to his message; he asked, "If you will, turn back a few pages to Romans chapter three, and verse twenty-three. It says, 'For all have sinned, and fall short of the glory of God.' Now, most times when this verse is preached, the pastor, teacher, whatever, will stop there. That to me is a scare tactic. I'm not going to stop there! Keep reading the next three verses. It says, 'being justified freely by His grace through the redemption that is in Christ Jesus, whom God set forth as a propitiation by His blood, through faith to demonstrate His righteousness, because in His forbearance God has passed over the sins that were previously committed, to demonstrate at the present time His righteousness, that He might be just and the justifier of the one who has faith in Jesus.'

"So far, I have given you evidence as to why we are not to worry, assurance in our salvation, and how to get your own salvation if you are not yet born again. Remember when I said earlier that none of us are guaranteed tomorrow? Turn to Romans chapter six, verse twenty-three; I'm just about finished. Romans 6:23 says, 'For the wages of sin is death, but the gift of God is eternal life in Christ Jesus our Lord.'

Billy closed his Bible, and bowed his head; he was either gathering his next thought or he was praying. Maybe God was talking to him. When he looked up, he said, "Everyone in here is going to live forever. That's a fact. It is up to you how you choose to spend eternity. You don't hear it too often, maybe you never have, but if you die without Christ, instead of an eternity in Heaven with Jesus and the saints, you will spend eternity in hell with Satan and his demons! In Heaven, you will interact with other believers. In hell, you will be all alone. For eternity. Think about that for just a moment! Try to picture such a gruesome image in your mind. If you have never received Jesus Christ as your personal Savior, now is the time! You don't have to speak any fancy prayer or know a bunch of legal mumbo-jumbo; just say what is on your heart! Just confess your sins, all of the things in your life that has kept you from Him. Believe that He was crucified and shed His blood to cleanse you from your unrighteousness and on the third day, he rose from the grave, and He still lives today! He is at the right hand of God, making intercession for us! He will strip away all your sins! And He forgets them! Hallelujah! We can't forget them, but we are forgiven from them!"

Billy again paused in his message. He finished by saying, "I'll close with this: you will not have drugs in hell, so why not give them up now? There will not be any alcohol in hell, so why not give it up now? There will not be any pornography in hell, there will not be any sex in hell; so why not give up the adulterous lifestyle now? If you're thinking about what your friends will say, forget about them! They will have to stand before the Lord someday, as well! If they are true friends, they will support you, maybe even obtain their salvation by the words you share with them! If you lose those friends, you will have many more and better friends in the family of God! Please, don't fight that tugging at your heart; don't put it off because you may never get another chance!"

As Matthew watched this scene unfold, he heard his thoughts as he sat in the pew and bowed his head, "Lord, how can I live this life and be an attorney? Aren't they considered evil? Did I choose the wrong career? It's too late to change it now! Show me how I can live this life and be a successful attorney at the same time!" Matthew realized that he was not very successful in his pursuit of an answer to his questions.

Eighteen

After the service, Jacob and Natalie went home, while Matthew and Mandy went to the pizzeria to get lunch to take home. While driving there, Mandy turned to Matthew and asked, "Well, what did you think of Billy's message this morning?"

Matthew thought for a moment, then he replied, "It was one of the best that I have heard in a while! But, as you can probably remember, he always told stories in a way to keep our attention when he taught us in youth class!"

Mandy charged, "It is probably the only message you've heard in a while! Matty, I am worried"-

Matthew interrupted, "Hah! You're not supposed to worry, remember what Billy said?"

Mandy corrected her comment. "Okay, okay, then I'm deeply concerned about you, Matty! I love you! I'm going to miss you something awful when you go to New York; I won't be able to nag you about giving your life to Jesus! I want you to be with me forever, Matty! Don't you want to be with me forever, too?"

Matthew confessed while laughing, "I don't know! Sometimes you can be a pain in the butt!"

Mandy slapped his shoulder. "All right, I won't say another word about it while you're home! But promise me this: you will seriously think about it? And you will take the Bible I got you to New York with you? Promise me that you will at least make an attempt to read it every day?"

Matthew sighed and smiled softly, "I promise I'll try; I can't promise I will!"

Mandy smiled slightly. She was always thinking of her brother and his salvation. Once she accepted Jesus as her Lord and Savior, she has been a bundle of confidence; she was confident of herself before, but now she feels as if there is nothing impossible. She feels as if she can do anything she chooses and if she has the Lord's blessing to pursue it.

Matthew admired that about her. He remembers wishing he could be that confident and worry free about everything in his life. He realizes now he has no life to wish to change.

"I suppose it's futile to ask for a break, or maybe a drink of water?" Matthew asked. He waited for a response, and received none. "That's what I thought." He solemnly answered.

The next year of his life was lived at an arduous pace. He was becoming familiar with the firm, his colleagues, New York laws, big city traffic, and just the differences between Durham, North Carolina and New York City. It's like a state itself!

He had now reached the time in his life that he does not want to see ever again; he can still see it all too vividly without the review playing it for him. It was September 10, 2001; Matthew had just got home from a dinner and drinks with some of his friends and colleagues at Hero's Sports Bar and Grill. It was almost 10:00 PM; he had no idea that this would be the last night he would see some of his friends.

His telephone started ringing almost immediately after he placed his keys on the table by the door. He remembers this call well. It was his sister Mandy. This was the call that, every time he reflects upon the foresight and prudence of it, still sends tremors up his spine. It seemed like days ago he received the call; not the years that have passed. He was lost in the memories of the series of events that were about to happen; he was not paying close attention to the conversation he had with Mandy that night. Until his attention was, as if supernaturally, returned to the screen.

"Matty, I'm not going to keep you much longer; I know you can take care of yourself. But please, think about this: have I ever just called to warn you before? Think about when you were going through college; how many times did I call you to tell you I was praying for you, only to find out later when we talked that there were things that happened that made you wish you would have listened to your baby sister, your intelligent, baby sister? Well, I'm older now, and I listen to the spirit in me more closely now than I did then! I guess you could say I'm not as stubborn as I once was! I'm telling you; I am very serious! I've not felt an uneasiness in my spirit like this before! And don't tell me not to pray for you and that you will be okay! You're wasting your breath! You know, you can just surrender your life to Christ right now and I would not ever have to be concerned about your well being again, well, I mean, not on that level anyway!" Mandy orated.

"Mandy, I told you; I am too busy right now! I've only been here what, a little over a year? As soon as things are not so hectic, and you can pull yourself away from the hospital, we will find a Bible-believing church here in New York, and I will faithfully attend! That is, if you want an all-expense paid vacation in New York, even if you have to stay with your old brother!" Matthew professed.

Still, Mandy pleaded with him, "Matty, what if tomorrow doesn't get here? We are not guaranteed another day; we are not even given the assurance of our next minute! Oh, never mind, I'll stop preaching to you! You know, you are lucky to have a sister that loves you so much! I'm going to do my part; now, it's up to you, too! If something doesn't feel right tomorrow, don't do it! Just humor me, all right? And you can call me tomorrow and tell me what an over protector I am, or, you can call me to say, 'I'm sorry! You were right, I was wrong!' When was the last time you said that?"

"I can't remember! And, I promise! Thanks for calling. Tell Mom and Dad hello and I love them, and I will call them soon!" Matthew replied.

After hanging up the phone, Matthew took a shower and went immediately to bed. Tomorrow was a busy day, as his appointment calendar was full; in fact, it started at 8:00 AM and the last meeting scheduled is at 7:00 PM. He wanted to get a good night's sleep so he can be mentally at his best tomorrow.

Tuesday morning, September 11, 2001, began as many of the others. It was a beautiful summer morning in the city; the sun was shining brightly and there were very few clouds in the sky. Matthew was driving to work when the messenger service at his office called him on his cell phone. He turned down the stereo in his Porsche and answered his call. "Good morning, Matthew Craig speaking!" he answered.

"Mr. Craig?" a pleasant voice greeted him. "Your 8:00 breakfast appointment at Windows on the World cancelled; there was an illness in the family, and I have tentatively rescheduled for next Tuesday pending your court docket. Fortunately, for you they cancelled, as your 10:00 court hearing is now on the docket at 8:30 due to last minute settlements. If you have your files, you could go directly to the court. Have a good morning, Mr. Craig! We'll see you after court!"

Matthew turned off his phone, and proceeded to the courthouse parking. He arrived there at 8:15, allowing him time to review his notes for any last minute advantage he may gain. The case before his took longer than anticipated;

it could have began on time, but due to the volatility of the previous case, the judge had ordered a fifteen minute recess to begin after the courtroom was cleared.

It was supposed to be a simple plea entry; however, there was outbreak in the crowd at the proceedings. Apparently, according to the bailiff residing on the case, the accused was facing multiple charges. He was charged with four counts of rape, four counts of first-degree murder, three counts of second-degree murder, two counts of sodomy, and two counts of assault on a police officer. There were several angry members of the victims' families there, and they were ready to try and convict him, as well as issue his punishment.

Matthew glanced at his watch. It was 8:50. He could hear several sirens screaming nearby. The recorder came in the room and told everyone a plane has just crashed into the north tower of the World Trade Center. We also informed that our case would be delayed a little longer, as the judge was in a conference call. Shortly after 9:00, many of us heard what we thought was an explosion; seconds later, the recorder that informed us of the plane crash in the north tower, came racing into the room; she was as white as snow. She was hysterical; she informed us that a plane just crashed into the south tower, and that it had been deliberate. There is panic everywhere in the city. While we were still trying to contain our thoughts, a police officer came in and informed us that all business in this courthouse is suspended until further notice, and we were to evacuate immediately in an orderly but expedient manner.

Matthew made it to his car and headed home. It was like a mouse going through a maze; many of the streets were closing and many were blocked. His ten-minute commute from the courthouse to his apartment took thirty minutes. When he arrived home, he didn't bother closing the door behind him. He turned on his television to watch the news coverage of all the events. That is when he learned that the Pentagon was also a victim of a plane crash; American Airlines flight 77 crashed into it at 9:43, only moments ago. As he continued to watch in horror, it only became worse.

He had gone to the refrigerator to get a beer; he was only gone a minute. When he sat down on his sofa, he saw the south tower collapse. He felt as if his life was draining from him. As he tried in vain to absorb all of the unspeakable videos that were unfolding on the television, they announce that another plane, United Airlines 93 has crashed in Pennsylvania.

"Oh, my God, what is happening?" Matthew screamed loudly. He knew he needed a stronger drink. He grabbed one of the glasses at the bar, placed some ice cubes in it and poured it full of his favorite scotch. He took a huge drink, and then took a deep breath. He sat back down on the sofa and placed his drink on the table next to him. At 10:28, the north tower began to collapse. Matthew was paralyzed with anguish; he tried calling his parents, but his telephone was dead. He grabbed his cell phone to check for a signal. Yes! It was weak, but it would allow him to get through!

"Hello, Mom? Hey, have you been watching T.V.?" Matthew asked.

"Yes, Mandy called us!" Natalie said. "Are you all right?"

"Yes, I'm fine! Listen, I can't talk long; I do not know how long my cell will keep a signal, and our landlines are down right now! Please call Mandy to let her know that I am fine and I am home!" Matthew requested.

"Yes, yes, I will! Oh, praise God you are safe! Mandy had us all praying for you last night and again this morning! I tell you, that girl is a gift from God! She is a blessing!" Natalie testified.

"She sure is, Mom! I gotta go! I'll call you as soon as I can, okay? I love you! Tell Dad and Mandy I love them, too!" Matthew said.

"I will! God is great, isn't He, Matthew? You are blessed! Thank God for your blessings and His grace and mercy on your life today!" Natalie stipulated.

Matthew continued to watch the events as they unfolded. He learned that all state offices officially closed at 10:57; as far as he was concerned, they closed the moment the second tower attack occurred.

Nineteen

His afternoon consisted of alternating between five to ten minute naps and watching the tragedy that had befallen his city. He had decided to go out to get something to eat around 5:30, shortly after Building 7 collapsed from fire and from the debris of the towers. Most of the restaurants were sending food to the fire and rescue teams at what some are now calling "Ground Zero". He was numb; he couldn't concentrate. His thoughts were with his small circle of friends and colleagues that worked in the towers. Some of the news commentaries were saying this was the beginning of a global war. Many of the churches in the area were holding candlelight vigils; they wanted to pray for the victims and their families, the volunteers, the fire departments, the police officers, the medical personnel, and our country.

Matthew finished his meal and began his journey home. His return route took him past three churches. One was participating in a candlelight vigil; the other two were having prayer services indoors. They, too, had people outside with candles; all the pews inside well at full capacity. "Humph!" Matthew thought aloud. "It's too late to be praying for us to avoid military conflict! And if they are praying for a survivor, that's a hopeless prayer!"

As he approached the last church, he thought he recognized two of the people standing outside. As he got closer, he confirmed his original assessment. It was two of the brokers from the investment company in the building next door to his. There were also a couple of the secretaries from his own firm there with them. "You guys have about as much chance getting your prayers heard as I do!" Matthew continued with his conversation with himself. "Knowing those two guys as I do, I'd bet I've been to church more in the last five years than they have the last ten!"

Matthew watched his life replay as if it wasn't his; he didn't remember any of those events. He didn't remember very much from that week at all. He didn't remember being so judgmental; he sounded so self-righteous it even made him nauseous! "I should have been there! I am sure that I was acquainted with many of them; I was only thinking of myself!" Matthew thought. "Where was my compassion; where was my sympathy? My God, I was a poor excuse of a human being! Was I the only one that internalized everything I was feeling? Was I the only one that chose to be alone?"

Once again, he heard the words of his pastor, "Judge not, lest ye be judged." Why is it that now he can hear or recall all of the things he had learned in church throughout the years? Having admitted he could not remember many of the events of that time, the next scene was an eye-opening, life-altering moment. He was back at his apartment; he was still watching updates and any breaking news as it happened. Suddenly, he saw himself falling to his knees. He heard his unremembered prayer. "God, why did this evil happen to so many good people? Is this the beginning of the end? Why do I feel so alone? Why did I lose my only friends here? What have I done; am I being punished? Where do I find my answers to all of these questions? Are you even going to answer me?"

He checked his cell phone; now recharged, he could make calls. Before he could, it began to ring. He quickly answered it. "Hello!" he said expectantly.

"Hey, big brother, how are you holding up?" Mandy asked empathetically. "I can't imagine how things are there! Is it safe for you to stay there? I mean, with all the smoke, the fumes of burning fuel, and God only knows what else in the air? Will your work be suspended for a few days?"

"Always firing the questions like a machine gun! Do you ask your patients this many questions this fast? They are gonna be confused!" Matthew attempted to hide his disquiet by joking. "I'm okay, now that you have called! Yes, the smell is terrible; the air is a plume of grey dust, smoke, debris, and ashes. I have not heard anything about my case schedule; I would assume they will clear the dockets for a couple of days, but you never can tell. I think I am going to stay here regardless of what happens; I mean, I can't get on a plane and come home!"

"Were you ever in any danger today? Are you now?" Mandy asked anxiously.

Matthew realized the gravity of his situation as soon as she finished her question. He fell back into the sofa. He gasped for a breath. "No, but...I should have been. I had a breakfast appointment at 8:00 AM at Windows on the World, but he cancelled. Then, my 10:00 AM court hearing moved up to 8:30, and then delayed after I arrived at the courthouse. It was while I was at the courthouse that all hell broke loose. Mandy, I should have been in that tower! I should be dead! If it weren't for a family illness that cancelled my appointment, I"-

Mandy interrupted, "You stop right there! Have you not listened to any of the things I've taught you? God has a purpose for your life! It's probably safe to say that He has a purpose for the life of that man that cancelled on you! God may have used him in order to protect you, if that was His plan! If you would have been there, you could not fulfill the call on your life!"

"Mandy, what could God possibly want me to do? I'm an attorney remember? Aren't we supposed to be evil or something?

Matthew again made a futile attempt at humor. "Seriously Mandy, I am not as well versed in His Word as you, and I don't see how I could do whatever it is in New York!"

"Who says it will happen in New York?" Mandy asked incredibly. "Your future may be somewhere else; this may be a training ground in which He molds you and uses the experiences you gain here to take with you to be an effective tool!"

Matthew shrugged, "I know you believe everything you just said, but I cannot comprehend why He would use me instead of someone who is more qualified."

"Let me answer that question with a question. Did you just decide you were going to be an attorney and the next day you started trying cases?" Mandy queried.

"Well, that is a stupid question," Matthew replied. "You know I had to go to college! I had to bust my rear to get the grades and then again to pass the bar exam! And then I had to hope to land a good job with an established firm!"

"Okay then, don't you think that maybe, just maybe, that God is training you while you are oblivious to all of it?" Mandy inquired.

"I thought I was supposed to be the one that gave the advice and shared the wisdom?" Matthew questioned.

Mandy confidently replied, "I guess I just have to live with being wiser than my big brother! It will be a struggle, but I must strive on!"

"All right, enough! But really though, I am so glad you called! I've felt disoriented with everything that's happened; I've felt alone, almost lost. You always know how to make me feel better, even if you always preach to me!" Matthew admitted.

Mandy shot back quickly, "I don't always preach! Besides, I am not the one saying the things that make you feel better, I mean, I'm saying it, but it's what He's telling me to tell you! God is consoling you and comforting you! If He is bringing you this much peace now, just imagine how much greater it will be once you are His child!"

"You will never give up, will you?" Matthew wearily asked.

"Nope, not a chance! I love you too much! Aren't you lucky to have me?" Mandy continued.

Matthew divulged, "Oh, I'm so blessed to have you for a sister!"

Mandy cheerfully answered, "See? God revealed that to you! You are blessed!"

Matthew responded, "I think this is a good time to end this conversation! Give Mom and Dad my love! I'll talk to you soon! I love you, too, you know?"

"Yeah, I know! I love you, too, Matty! Good night!" Mandy replied.

"Good night, Mandy!" Matthew responded, smiling.

After turning off his phone, Matthew took a shower and went to bed. He knew there was nothing he could do about the events that have unfolded. He was not used to having no control over situations in his life. He could not wrap his mind around the magnitude of the day's events. He needed to release his mind of all the terror, panic, death, the ugliness. Maybe he will see things more clearly after a good night of rest; he couldn't see how he would find rest tonight in a city that was presiding in unrest tonight.

Matthew woke up to his apartment telephone ringing. It was confirmation of what he suspected last night; the firm's offices will be closed the remainder of the week, and all court hearings have been postponed and will be rescheduled later.

This meant that he had the whole day to think, to reflect. He could spend the day trying to see the purpose of the senselessness of this attack. He took a quick shower to help him wake up. After he finished getting dressed, he walked down to ground zero. It was not a long walk for a former country boy, it just seemed longer in the city. The time walking allowed him quiet time to think; he found himself talking to God again. This is two days in a row; that has not happened in... well, he can't remember the last time.

"Lord, why did this happen? Why is it that everyone waits until the tragedy has happened before they come to you? I know that I am not alone in that category! I would bet most of them were working 70 hours a week! What for... an early retirement, a bigger bank account? If it is all for nothing, if it doesn't matter anyway, why try? What about all of the families and friendships that were lost, destroyed, in one moment? I lost no family, but I lost friends! And I cannot stand the hurt, the loss!" Matthew stopped walking for a moment. There was still dust and smoke in the air; the closer he got to the site the more pronounced it become. He closed his eyes and lifted his head to the sky. He released a mournful sigh, and then pledged, "I will not let myself feel like this again! Starting next week, when I return to work, I'm going to be the best attorney this city has ever seen! I will be relentless; I will not fail, no matter the cost! I will protect my interests and my feelings! If I want something, I will get it! I will enjoy each day of this life while I have it!"

He continued walking until he reached a police officer at which time he volunteered any assistance he could provide. For the next three days, he spent ten hours a day passing out bottled water to the firefighters, paramedics, and police officers. When he returned home, he would work on his career agenda; he wanted a tangible reminder of his new life plan. After witnessing the sights and stories while at his volunteer station, he found motivation and incentive to complete his plan.

When Matthew announced his intentions at the weekly meeting, the senior partners were pleased; not only did this show them boldness, a hint of arrogance, but also revealed someone with a desire for success at any cost. Each of them saw a little piece of themselves when they were his age. They were also more than happy to accommodate to help him achieve his goals; two of their mid-level attorneys were lost in the attacks. To help jump start his plan, they moved him from the office he was sharing with another 'rookie'. He knew this person would never get very far in the company; he had no drive, no killer instinct. He was a very intelligent man, but his priorities were unorganized.

When Matthew reached his new office, he was very pleased. He had a window office! It was not one of the executive suites, but he had an office all to himself. He could arrange it how he saw fit. He did not want his desk in front of the window; he did not want to be like everyone else. The window was for looking at the scenery, allowing the sunlight and the moonlight to shine through. He loved looking at the sun and the moon when he had the opportunity; it was his temporary escape to New Hope, even if it was for only a few scarce seconds. It brought tranquility to a frantic schedule. He could now play his own preference of music on his stereo, as loud as he wanted and any time he wanted. Music always helped him think; it helped him focus. He would claim it was his way of meditating daily; those that did not appreciate his new attitude said that he was taking power naps. They were either jealous and did not want to admit their own lack of desire to succeed, or they did not possess the faculties to reach that level.

He now had a secretary. Her name was Janelle Parks. She was very smart; if she continues her education, she will be a formidable ally or opponent. She was also dangerously beautiful. She knew it, and she flaunted it. She worked out at the health club the firm had on the thirty-fifth floor, and her body was evidence of her dedication and her diligence to her workout regimen. She purchased clothes to reflect her professionalism and yet accentuate her assets. Today was especially difficult, as she was wearing a thin, white cotton shirt, and a bright pink skirt cut slightly above the knees. Her tan, her taut legs, and an ample amount of cleavage she readily made available each time she came into Matthew's office.

There was always an exchange of playful flirtation; both knew how far it could go without breaking any laws. Matthew would often find himself staring at her; he would watch her as she placed his cases and motions into the filing cabinet.

She seemed to know that he was watching her; she always positioned herself to allow him the best view. She was being a tease; it seemed to make the workday pass quicker and it was a lot less stressful for both of them. She always made sure when she would go into his office with his messages or any research information that he had requested, she would either hand them to him by standing in front of his desk leaning in towards him, or directly beside him to allow the slightest physical contact.

Matthew noticed it; many others at the firm noticed it, too. It was a hot subject for several weeks when they had their weekly staff meetings in the war room on Monday mornings. The questions he had to answer were usually the same, from, "Did you uncover any new evidence this weekend, Matthew?" or, "Did you and your secretary prepare any oral statements?" then there was, "I hear your secretary has some assets she would like for you to evaluate!"

If this was all they had to discuss with him, that was fine with him. After all, he was winning every nickel and dime case they threw at him. He wanted bigger fish to fry. He was ready for a shark. This Monday, he got his wish. It was a securities fraud indictment, and the client was facing jail time of up to twenty years and fines in excess of a million dollars. The senior partners all agreed that I was ready for the big boys. It was now time for me to land the big one to begin my path to recognition, wealth, and respect among the elite group.

Twenty

ℒℐ

H̲e later discovered he was taking a case nobody else
wanted to take. Janelle told him, "I was talking with
the other secretaries at lunch and that they had told her that
the senior partners 'didn't care if this idiot goes to jail! He's
an embarrassment to the firm! The only reason he is a client
is because his father was a respected client for over thirty
years, and when he took over for his Dad, their contract with
the firm was still binding for another five years!' Janelle
added, "You know, that would be more incentive to win, if
it was me! If I was given a case I couldn't win, or I wasn't
expected or even supposed to win, I would take advantage
of any help I could get to prove my intellect and ability to
win any case!"

"Does that mean you are prepared to work long hours to
help me win this thing?" Matthew asked. "You know, you
could possibly use this case as a topic for a thesis or a case
discussion in one of your courses in the future!"

Janelle looked at him quizzically, "What do you mean,
my courses? I'm not in college anymore!"

Matthew stumbled apologetically over his words, "I'm
sorry! I just assumed that with your intelligence and your

fierce determination that you were planning to become an attorney in the future!"

Janelle smiled, "Do you think I could? If you are trying to seduce me by complimenting my intelligence, it's not working! Besides, if you want me, all you have to do is ask!"

Matthew, taken aback by her response, tried to hide the smile he felt rising up from within him. He responded, "Janelle, you know that can't happen! We would both lose our jobs, and we would never work in the city again! But, when you pass your bar exam, you let me know! We will celebrate in style! I'll determine where we have our dinner; you can determine where we have desert. Is that fair, counsel-to-be?"

Janelle readily agreed, "That's sounds terrific, Matthew. But, now I have a confession to make. It may be a conflict of interests in telling you this; promise me that my job is safe after I tell you this!"

Intrigued, yet also somewhat concerned, Matthew replied, "Will you need an attorney? How serious is your crime?"

Janelle pushed on his shoulder and divulged, "It's not a crime; however, it could be, I guess, in the company guidelines and code of ethics. I've been taking an on-line course to help me achieve attorney status. This will allow me to take my bar exam three months sooner."

"So where's the crime? Where is the misconduct?" Matthew asked bewilderingly.

Janelle confessed, "I've been taking my course while I'm here at work; but it is always when you are at court or have appointments outside the office! I have never let it interfere with my duties as your secretary!"

Matthew allowed his countenance turn solemn. He could see the apprehension on Janelle's face, and especially in her eyes. Finally, he declared, "Well, I guess you know what this means." He paused, then he took a deep breath and as he exhaled, he emitted a heavy sigh. He was giving it all of the theatrical effects he could; he affectionately wanted to let her anxiety percolate for a moment. "If you continue to take these courses while you are at work, while I'm gone, even though they do not affect your performance in any matter whatsoever, and I attest to that statement... I guess that I have to let you go..." He looked at her and seen the color drain from her face. Her body reacted as a balloon that just lost significant air supply. "...on doing it so you can reach your career goal sooner!"

Instantly the color returned to her beautiful face, and her shapely body once again stood straight and confident. "That was mean! It was good... but it was mean! Can you teach me to do that? It will be a good tactic to have in my arsenal in the courtroom!"

Matthew could not remember the incident that just happened, but he did remember Janelle. He remembers she did pass the bar, and she resigned shortly afterwards. However, she was there long enough to share in his victory in winning the securities fraud case that was "not winnable". Moreover, he even got his client back pay owed to him, with interest, and he even negotiated a compensatory settlement for his client's damaged reputation and negative media exposure. This was a perfect occasion to celebrate!

They never had the celebration he had mentioned, but they did share a lasting memory. On her last day, he did give her an extravagant gift, thanked her for her faithful and unrelenting support; she gave up too much of her personal life to help him win many of his cases. He can see now that it was preparation for the career she was about to begin. The kiss they shared was short; but it was sweet, tender, and loving. He wished her a happy and successful life, and then she was gone.

However, he did not have time to miss a great assistant or a good friend. He needed another secretary, because he was now a renowned attorney at the firm; and he was becoming more prominent attorney in New York. Two years in the Big Apple and he has reached the status that many dream about and never reach.

The senior partners knew they had a volatile situation on their hands; what could they offer this inestimable asset they have on their staff to attenuate him? They could not make him a partner; nobody becomes a partner before they are forty, much less thirty! If they could not make a very appealing, as well as very lucrative, offer, too many firms would love to see a black mark on Steele, Gold, and Rich; they would literally sell their soul to achieve that level of success, and would be willing to pay handsomely to see that occur.

They knew Matthew would have a profusion of offers, and very soon. He may have secretly already received offers. They did not waste any time. Before the end of the day on Friday, the senior partners held a meeting with Matthew. They were blunt; they knew that he valued time as much or more than they did. Mathew sat calmly as they talked of his accolades and his impossible victories. They wanted to let him know he was wanted as well as needed at Steele, Gold, and Rich. They handed Matthew the paper with their offer.

When Matthew opened the once-folded paper, he could not believe what he saw. He hid his expressions; he had become very adept at this valuable asset in his repertoire. The offer was more than even his lofty goals. If the offer was accepted, he would gain the vacant seat in their brokerage house, he would receive a monthly salary of $100,000, an expense account that fluctuated with the nature of his cases, an executive suite, an assistant in addition to his secretary; he could if he chooses to do so, keep his present secretary.

Finally, in addition to all of this, he would receive a bonus of $10,000 on every case in which he successfully tries.

Matthew studied the words on the page a second time. He set the paper down on the desk, and leaned back into his chair. He looked directly into the eyes of each of the men setting across from him. After stalling long enough, he leaned forward and said, "This is a very fair, actually, a very generous offer; but there was one thing I wanted that is not mentioned."

Mr. Steele interrupted him, "Son, there is no way we can offer you a partnership! It's just not done at your age!"

Matthew assured him, "Calm down, Mr. Steele! You don't want to let your anger be evident to those around you, or was that defensive retaliation?"

The other members laughed out loud. "How could you possibly want more? You have one hell of an offer there in front of you! That is more than 90% of the staff here; several of which, I might add, have several years, several years of seniority on you!" Mr. Steele bellowed. "What the hell more could you possibly want?"

"Careful there, Mr. Steele", Matthew calmly answered. "Outburst like that will give your opponent the upper hand. You want to win this case don't you? Let me finish what you interrupted me from saying earlier. There is one thing that is not in this offer; it would make this a done deal. I want to be able to expand my automobile collection, and I want to have access to the names of the people I need to see in order to obtain the same discounts that you, the senior partners, receive. Do you think that could be arranged?"

Matthew could not believe how calmly he responded. He could not believe he was asking for more! The salary alone amounts to a million dollar raise! He will go from his "meager" $300,000 annual salary to over $2,000,000, as he confidently added in bonuses he would be claiming.

Mr. Gold looked over his small, gold-rimmed glasses at Matthew and said, "It takes some big brass ones to sit there and do what you just did! Hell, how do you think I got where I am today? I was a damn lot older than you before I got an offer like this!" He took off his glasses and took a cloth out of his pocket to clean them. He too, knew how to pause for effect and build tension. He finished cleaning his glasses and slowly put them back on. He then turned his focus back to Matthew. "I respect a man that knows what he wants and is not afraid to say it! And damn, if you did it without showing any emotion! You are one hard-nosed S.O.B.!" He once again paused, and then he laughed heartily. "I'll give you the names of the man to see at Exotic Autos; he can find you any vehicle you want!" He then stood up and extended his arm to shake Matthew's hand. I guess we have a deal!"

Matthew stood up and allowed a smile to develop on his face. After shaking the hand of each partner, he excused himself and went back to his office to get some files to take home with him to review over the weekend. When he arrived at his car, his excitement could wait no longer. He grabbed his cell phone and called his parents.

Natalie answered, as always. "Hello?" she answered in her usual sweet, loving voice.

"Hi, Mom! How are things at home?" he asked.

"Oh hi, Matt! Everything's fine! Your Dad just got home from work a few minutes ago! Mandy was off today. She has been watching television and taking naps all day. Your sister has been working tirelessly lately! Are you still at work?" she questioned rapidly. He now understands where Mandy got this trait.

"No, I just left the office. Hey, the reason I'm calling, well when is Dad planning on retiring?" he wondered.

"Oh, honey, you know your Dad! He would love to do other things; he's got a lot of honey-do projects he needs to get done here at the house; he is more involved with the

'Haven for the Homeless' the men at the church started last year. Besides, things at work are more stressful; he won't admit to it, but I can tell when he comes home some nights. Why on earth are you asking about this?" she inquired.

"What if I told you that Dad could afford to retire now if he wanted?" Matthew offered. "Would he do it? How much would it take?"

Natalie laughed loudly. "Why, did you win the lottery or something?"

Matthew was about to explode he wanted to tell them so desperately. "No, it was no lottery. I just got a raise today!" he revealed.

Twenty-One

⌒∞⌒

A lways the mother, Natalie advised, "Matthew Craig! We taught you better! You need to save for your future! We will be fine! You best not be spending that money; you will need it down the road! What if another 9/11 happens and you are out of work for a while?"

Matthew responded, "I guess I'll come home and aggravate you and Dad for a while!"

Her curiosity has now peaked. "Matt, you are acting very strange, even more than usual! What is going on?"

"I told you; I got a raise today!" he repeated to her. "And I think that I can help you and Dad; you can finally do some of the things you didn't get to do because you were too busy raising me and Mandy! Take a vacation, take two vacations; buy yourselves something you want, not just something you need! Whatever you or Dad want, just say it! I want to do something great for both of you; it's the least I can do for everything you've done for me! I couldn't have gotten where I am now if it weren't for the two of you; all of your help, encouragement, love, and sacrifices."

"Well, that's just what a parent is supposed to do; besides, we wanted to do it! We want you and Mandy to have it easier than we did! We want you to have a better life" Natalie shared.

"I thought we had a pretty good life, Mom!" Matthew responded hesitantly. "Were you not happy; are you not happy?"

Natalie quickly corrected herself, "Oh God, Matthew, I didn't mean that! What I meant was if we would have been better off financially, we could have given you and Mandy more! You certainly wouldn't have needed to pay for any of your college expenses; you would not have even needed to help pay for your sister's education! This is something that the parent should do!"

"You and Dad could not have done anything more or anything better; except maybe made the whippings a little less painful!" Matthew lovingly encouraged her. "Hey Mom, I've got somewhere I need to go; so, how about it? What would you and Dad like to do? Come on and tell me!"

"Oh, Matt! Well, if we're going to play this game, then let's finish it! Do you remember when Dad said when he retired, he wanted to raise a big garden and sell the surplus to make some extra cash; you know, something to occupy his time?" Natalie asked. "Well, he is going to need a tractor, he'll need all of the attachment thingies that go with it, he will need a truck to haul all of the vegetables in from the garden, and let's see, what else will he need? Well, he will need one of those gas tanks and pumps that the farmers have so they can have fuel for their equipment. Did I forget anything?"

"Well, that's good for Dad! What about you? What would you like?" Matthew asked.

"Well, I want a kitchen that will cook supper for me!" Natalie joked. "I don't know; how about new kitchen appliances and a new washer and dryer? Oh, and how about a new television, too?"

"That sounds good, for starters!" Matthew replied. "I'll see what I can do!"

"Always dreaming big, aren't you, Matt?" Natalie commented.

"What's the use in trying if you don't have a dream? So, you may as well dream big!" Matthew answered philosophically. "I've got to go! I'll call you tomorrow! Tell Dad and Mandy I love them!"

"We love you, too, Matt! Good-bye!" Natalie replied.

Matthew spent the next two weeks working frantically in order to clear his schedule for a week of vacation. His new office would not be ready until the Monday he would return from vacation, so it would work out perfectly. When he had a free moment between cases, he was making phone calls to collect all of the necessary pieces of the wish list puzzle his mother had given him. He also had to order his plane ticket to fly home; he needed to call Mandy to pick him up at the airport. She could keep a secret; he did not want his parents to know he was coming home for a week. He did not tell Mandy what he was planning to do; no one knew of his plan to fulfill his parents' wishes. She also did not know of a little detour he was planning for her, as well. He had accomplished everything on his personal agenda by the end of business on Wednesday; this allowed him time to pack his things on Thursday evening and relax on Friday evening before flying home on Saturday morning.

His flight was one of the smoothest flights he can recall; he was looking forward to a week of relaxation and spending time with his family. He was also looking forward to seeing the reaction of his parents when their gifts arrive on Monday. Mandy was already at the airport waiting for him. He ran to give her a hug; he could not believe how much she has changed. Her intelligence and confidence radiated from her beauty. He grabbed his luggage and followed her to the car. After they were loaded and ready to go, he informed her they had a couple stops to make before going home.

"I'm not going to be your chauffer while you're here, brother!" Mandy announced.

"And I don't expect you to! Trust me, these stops are vitally important!" Matthew assured her. "Let's go to Piggly Wiggly first; I want to load up with our favorites! I know you have to work, but you will be home sometimes, so let's be bad this week! Besides, I want some steaks and burgers for the grill!"

"We haven't used the grill in years, Matty! It probably will not work-wait a minute, Dad gave it away last fall!" Mandy informed him.

"Well, I guess we have to buy a grill! So, if you don't care, let's go to Home Depot first!" Matthew declared.

"Mom said you have been acting strange! I mean, you always were strange, but more than normal!" Mandy revealed. "Do you care to share what is up with you?"

"Didn't Mom tell you?" Matthew asked. "I got a raise; I also got an unexpected bonus that I didn't get the chance to tell her about yet! Do they know that you were coming after me? Did you tell them?"

"No, it's still a surprise; I made my pager go off and told them I had to go out for a couple of hours." Mandy stated.

"Good! Well, let's get this party started! I'm on vacation! Let's have some fun!" Matthew implored.

While at the Home Depot purchasing the biggest and best grill they had in stock, Mandy noticed his conversation with the store manager. She assumed he was someone Matthew knew or remembered from his college days.

"So, it's no problem to move the Craig delivery up to late this afternoon instead of Monday? I will give you and the deliverymen a bonus if you make it happen! I did not know about the grill until I arrived here from New York; I don't want to make you drive out there twice! I deeply appreciate this!" Matthew shared sincerely.

The two men shook hands and exchanged smiles. Mandy assured herself that she was right; they were simply old friends. Matthew was all smiles as he exuberantly walked towards her. Everything was going more perfectly than he could've planned.

"Now, we have to hurry! We still need to go to the store to make my last stop!" Matthew declared excitedly. "Aren't you excited?"

"You are weirding me out, Matty!" Mandy protested. "What has gotten in to you?"

"Let's just say, my hard work has paid off, and my hard work is just beginning", Matthew answered mysteriously. "Mandy, I've got to tell you now; I can't wait until we get home! I was going to tell all of you together, but I know you will act surprised when I tell them! My raise, Mandy, was not just a raise; I got a promotion, you might say."

"Well congrats, Matty!" Mandy offered. "How much dough are you going to be rolling in now, moneybags? Did I mention that I could use a new car?"

"Well, even if you didn't ask nicely, I guess I'll tell you", Matthew said. "I'm going to be going back to school myself, you might say; I am going to be a stockbroker in my spare time! And guess what else? This time next year, I will officially be a millionaire!"

Mandy rolled her eyes and laughed, "Yeah, right, Matty; and I'm going to be driving a new Lexus and have my own parking space at the hospital!"

"Which Lexus do you want?" Matthew inquired.

Mandy chortled, "Does it matter?"

Matthew replied, "Why don't you drive by the dealership since it's on our way home and show me the one you like!"

"Don't you think we should hurry home?" Mandy asked. "I mean, it is officially your vacation now, right?"

"Hey, nobody knows I'm home except for you and my boss!" Matthew reminded her. "Since they think you went to the hospital, they expect nothing, right?"

Mandy muttered, "Yeah, but"-

"But what?" Matthew interrupted.

"It can be a little depressing to look at those fancy cars; it can be even more depressing to look at them and want one of them! So, as long as I don't look, I can't want; and I don't have to get depressed!" Mandy explained.

Matthew pleaded, "Do it for me, sis! We can pretend just like we used to do when we were kids! C'mon, it'll be fun! Besides, I want to see your taste in cars!"

Mandy sighed heavily. "All right, bro! You win; but you're gonna owe me!"

Matthew eagerly agreed, "You've got a deal!"

When they arrived at the dealership, one of the associates greeted Matthew. He turned to Mandy and said, "Go look and find the one you absolutely love; I'll be right there!"

After Mandy walked away, Matthew informed the associate that the sales manager should be expecting him; he told him his name, and the associate went to notify the manager. Moments later, the manager was walking out to greet him.

"Mr. Craig, it is a pleasure to meet you!" the manager announced. "My colleagues at our dealership in the Bronx have a valued owner named Mr. Gold that has requested we offer you our gold key service! Just let me know the vehicle you wish to obtain, and we will handle the rest!"

Matthew reached out to shake hands with the manager in agreement. As he turned to walk towards Mandy, she had apparently found the car she wanted. "Well, is this the dream car; is this the one you wish to be driving for a few years?" Matthew requested.

"Oh, my gosh, Matty, this one is perfect! It is the color I love, it has all the toys I want; it's got the GPS, the upgraded stereo package, the upgraded leather package...everything!"

Mandy announced enthusiastically. "The one next to it is more realistic, if I can say that with a straight face; it's the right color, and it is still a Lexus, it just doesn't have all the toys!" Mandy bleakly informed him. She shifted her focus just over Matthew's left shoulder to the activity going on at her car. She looked at Matthew alarmingly and asked, "Hey, where are they going with my car?"

Matthew assured her, "Oh, they're just cleaning it out for you; it's nothing to worry about!"

He had managed to get her to turn around to look at the car parked adjacent to the two that she had described to Matthew. When she turned to look, Matthew signaled to the manager the car he would be taking. The manager walked over to the area they were standing and said, "It looks as if this beauty has found a new home! I've got to take it to prep for a wash and a fill-up of the gasoline tank!"

Matthew turned to look at Mandy; she looked dejected, defeated. "Somebody has impeccable taste", Mandy disclosed. "Thanks, Matty; you managed to both excite me and depress me in the same minute! Let's go get my car and go to Piggly Wiggly!"

"That sounds like an excellent idea!" Matthew agreed. "Let's go in the showroom to see if they have your car cleaned out yet!"

Once in the showroom, Mandy was oblivious to Matthew's dealings, as she was enamored with the SUV that was there. It was not quite her color, but it was still beautiful. She shook her head and laughed, flabbergasted by her interest in such an impracticable vehicle. She turned to walk towards the area Matthew was standing. The manager and he were both smiling; she assumed they were sharing a humorous story. She could not have been more clueless!

Matthew turned to walk toward Mandy. He looked at her still obviously depressed countenance. "Your car will be back in a minute, and we can take off, okay? Hey, you still love your big brother, don't ya?"

"Yeah, I guess so", Mandy replied, managing to form a smile on her lovely face. "Somebody's got to, huh?"

"Yeah, I guess so, sis!" Matthew replied. "Here are your keys."

When she took her keys, she didn't pay attention to them; she knew instinctively by the feel of the keys they were not hers. She handed the keys back to Matthew, allowing her eyes to focus on them as she announced, "Matty, these aren't mine! These are the keys to one of their cars!"

Matthew took the keys, looked at them, then enlightened her, "Nope, these are the right keys!"

Mandy tried not to let her hope and excitement emanate; her eyes were brighter than Matthew could ever recall seeing them. "Matthew," she sobbed as the tears began to flow exceedingly, "this is not funny...are you saying"-

"That you have your dream car? If that's your question, then yes, that's what I'm saying!" Matthew interrupted.

Mandy embraced her brother tightly as she sobbed uncontrollably, while laughing with joy and happiness. "Thank you so-o-o-o very much, Matthew! I am so blessed to have a brother with such a big heart and a giving spirit! I love you!"

Twenty-Two

As Matthew watched a happy chapter in his life, a tear trickled down his cheek; he could not remember ever seeing Mandy this overjoyed! Wait, that's not right; she was always full of joy, she always seemed to be happy. But this happiness was a personal, dare he say, selfish happiness. He was glad that he was the only person that got to enjoy and share this moment with her. He continued to brush away the tears of happiness as they escaped from his eyes. He did not want this moment to pass, but he wanted to relive the same excitement that was about to come.

Mandy was almost afraid to get in her new car. When she finally sat down in the driver's seat, she caressed the steering wheel; she grabbed one of the compact discs that the dealership transferred from her old car into her new CD player. She started the car, but before driving away, she informed Matthew, "No eating or drinking in the car, you got it? If we need to, tell the bagger at the store to double bag our meat! Wait! Maybe we can buy a cooler to keep it in; that way it stays cold and my car is protected!"

Matthew smiled, "Yes, indeed! I understand clearly and completely!"

"Okay," Mandy acknowledged. "Let's get this done so we can get home! I can't wait to show my car to Mom and Dad!"

"And don't forget, surprise them by bringing me home with you!" Matthew added.

"Oh well, of course, Matty, I haven't forgot!" Mandy assured him.

It was the fastest Mandy had ever shopped with him, or so it seemed. Excitement and anticipation filled the trip home. Mandy was still having spells, alternating between crying and giggling. She continued with trying to push every button, turn every dial, inspecting and validating that everything worked as designed to work.

"Hey this is really cool, Matty! It even gives us directions to *our* house!" Mandy revealed, speaking of her GPS system.

The conversation and watching Mandy's expressions made the trip home pass quickly. Natalie stood on the porch, leaning against one of the posts, studying the strange car pulling in the driveway. She noticed Mandy first; maybe the enormous smile gave her away. The sun was shining on the passenger side of the car, therefore she could not figure out who her passenger was. When Matthew opened his car door and stepped out, Mandy had already reached her mother, hugging her as exuberantly as she had him earlier.

To say his mother was surprised was an understatement; she was thrilled to see the son that never visits because he never took any time away from work or took a vacation! This was the first time he had come home since the 9/11 attacks. She could tell he has been a different man since that day. His life now seemed defined by his work, driven to block out his feelings. She had once suggested he talk to someone, maybe try praying -for peace, wisdom, comfort- to help accept and live with what happened. Instead, he poured all of it into becoming a driven force to reckon with at his firm. However, he did look rather relaxed this morning. Hopefully this is the beginning of a change.

Matthew stood to let the sun penetrate his face, his arms, and his mind, all the way to his soul if it could. He lifted his eyes towards the sky and smiled.

As he began walking towards the house, he asked his mother, "Well, how do you like Mandy's new car?

Natalie walked to look at the reason for her excitement. "Yes, it is a beautiful car, Mandy; can you afford this? Maybe you should have gotten something more...practical!"

"But Mom, I didn't buy it; Matthew bought it for me!" Mandy professed. "His logic is, 'if it's your drive to be a doctor, you should arrive like a doctor!'. Matty, thanks again! Let me help you get your luggage from the car!"

"Luggage? What is this?" Natalie inquired. "What's going on, Matthew?"

"Well, my new office will not be finished before next Monday, my schedule is clear for the upcoming week, and I decided that I needed this free time to visit my family, recharge my batteries, so to speak, and to make up for all of the holidays and birthdays I have missed!" Matthew confessed.

"But", Natalie reminded, "You have always called and sent gifts; very extravagant gifts, I might add! Now you've went and bought...how can you afford this? You shouldn't spend your raise before you even earn it!"

"Mom, it's okay, honestly!" Matthew assured her. Just trust me, and be happy for me; be happy for Mandy!"

After he unpacked his things and had himself settled in, Matthew went to sit on the porch with his parents. His mom was relaxing on the swing, as was his dad. Jacob had just come in from doing some work in the barn. Natalie already had a glass of iced tea poured for him and had set it on the table that was within arm's reach of the swing.

When he first realized his son was home, his posture became erect, his gait quickened. Matthew walked out to meet his dad. They were never ashamed to hug each other; Matthew did not understand why, whenever a son hugging his father or any other male family member, many people stared or had the strangest expressions upon their faces. A handshake with someone you love, with family, seemed so cold to him. He loved his family; and, even though his frequent absence from family events would indicate otherwise, he was not ashamed to show that love and appreciation to them.

"Son, you're lookin' older than I do!" Jacob observed. "That's what that livin' in that big crazy city will do to ya!"

Matthew lamented, "Gee, thanks, Dad! You're looking great; I see your keen, unique sense of humor has gotten sharper!"

"Yes, I guess it has! Thank God for the satellite TV!" Jacob proclaimed. "The only thing that would be better would be one of those new, giant screened televisions that you can hang up on a wall just as if it were a picture or a painting! That would be great for football season!"

Natalie chided, "Daddy! Cut it out!"

"Well, if he can get his sister a fancy new car, he can get his good old dad a new television!" Jacob deduced.

"Sorry, Dad! I didn't realize you were that interested in one! You know, we can go to Circuit City, Best Buy, and Sears next week, look at some of the ones they have, and find one that you like!" Matthew enlightened.

Natalie butted in, "Matt, he does not need a big television! The one we have works just fine!"

"How old is that TV anyway, Mom?" Matthew asked.

"I don't know; Mandy do you remember when we got it?" Natalie asked.

"I think it was the Christmas before I graduated, Mom!" Mandy contemplated.

Matthew fired back quickly, "See there, Mom? It can go at anytime; you and Dad need a new television! Mandy can take us all into town and we can even have a family dinner after a day of shopping! How does that sound?"

Jacob and Mandy excitedly agreed, nodding their heads in approval; however, Natalie was determined to rain on their parade.

"Matt if we need to get a TV, we can get it ourselves! You better save your money!" she responded, muffling her sobs.

"Mom, I'm sorry I upset you; but, really, it's okay!" Matthew reiterated. "None of us will ever need to worry about our finances again! I mean, between Mandy and me, none of us will ever have to 'wait until we can afford it' again!"

"Matthew, have we not taught you anything?" Jacob asked. "Your mom has a valid point! Did we not always say the Lord will provide our needs? Did we ever go without food? Did we ever go without water, electricity, or any of our other basic needs? Aren't we commanded to seek the Kingdom of God first, and all these things will be added to us? It's never failed us!"

"Yes, but let me ask both of you this-doesn't His Word also say to ask for the desires of your heart? Aren't we to ask in His name to receive that our joy may be full? I can't quote verses; that's Mandy's job. Am I correct?" Matthew questioned. He looked each of them directly in their eyes. "Mandy? Mom? Dad? Is anyone going to respond?"

"Well, that's taking God's Word and interpreting it for your own benefit, Matt!" Natalie spoke up.

Matthew continued to press, "Aren't we supposed to take God at His word? Does He not want us to be happy? If you are obedient, following His Words and commandments, if you are working within the church to advance the Kingdom, if you are loving your neighbor as He instructed, why would he not want you to have things?"

There was silence on the porch; the breeze that began to blow was the only air moving between them. Everyone just looked at each other as if expecting the other to make a comment. Then, as if on cue, the sound of an approaching truck interrupted the silence.

Jacob wondered aloud, "What in the world would one of those big trucks be doing out here on a Saturday?"

Merely seconds after uttering that statement, the Home Depot truck topped the hill just beyond their house. "I wonder where they're going!" Natalie mused.

Mandy broke the silence. "They're just delivering the grill Matty bought! He said he wanted to have a cookout, and I told him we didn't have a grill anymore, so, here we are!" she revealed.

Matthew simply leaned back in his chair to enjoy the events about to unfold. After the truck had pulled in their driveway and parked, the man that verified the delivery invoices and assisted the driver in the unloading emerged from the truck and began to talk to no one in particular.

"Sure is a hot one today, ain't it folks? Uh, we got a delivery here for a Mr. and Mrs. Craig, is this the right place?" he asked. After seeing that his question was answered by a unity of positive nods, he continued, "You folks have great taste! These are the best appliances that we sell! These will last you forever, Mr. and Mrs. Craig!"

"Appliances!" Natalie gasped. "I thought we were getting a grill!"

"Oh, don't worry, Mrs. Craig, we got it on here, too!" the man assured her.

"Matt, what's going on?" Natalie asked her now devilishly smiling son.

Matthew replied, "Well, you said"-

"I also said not to spend your money!" Natalie interrupted him. "You need to save your money! It may all be gone tomorrow; and at the rate you're spending it, it's probably already gone!"

"Mom, just relax", Matthew attempted to explain. "Wait until they are finished and we can discuss it further!"

Her words may have said denial, but her eyes were saying acceptance. As they unloaded each of the stainless steel kitchen appliances, she looked excited, overjoyed, and even almost relieved. She knew in her heart that, even though all her appliances were still working properly, that is no guarantee they would be very much longer. They were becoming quite old; they had decided they would wait until one died before they would replace it. Now they will not have to worry about it anymore.

When they unloaded the washer and dryer, she became somewhat of a comedian. She slapped Matthew lovingly on the back of his shoulder and remarked, "I could have used those when both of you were in school! *Now* I get a really great washer and dryer! You even picked out a color to match the laundry room! You did a good job, Matt!"

"Does that mean you like your stuff? Am I now off the hook for spending my money how *I* wanted?" Matthew asked his mother. Before she answered, Matthew turned to his dad and confessed, "I'm sorry, Dad; I didn't want to let you know! I wanted to make everything just one big surprise!"

"What are you talking about?" Jacob asked curiously.

After removing the dryer, which everyone else thought was the last item, the two men went back into the back of the truck. As they were carrying it down the ramp, Matthew could see the puzzled look on his dad's face.

"I hope you like your new TV, Dad!" Matthew announced.

It was more than his parents could have imagined; it was a wonderful and welcome surprise for Mandy as well.

Matthew felt better than he had in, well, it has been too long for him to remember. He was feeling joy from knowing he could give his parents this little moment of happiness, and knowing it would make his mom's work in the kitchen a little easier. He was also feeling comfort in knowing they will avoid the financial burden of the expense of having to replace any household appliances. He was now ready to enjoy the rest of, though he would never admit it, his much-needed vacation. Even on vacation, he could not allow himself to show a weakness in his armor.

Matthew painfully watched what was supposed to be a happy memory in his life. He could only lower his head in disgust with himself for becoming so driven, so restless, so...cold. Thank God, his Mom and Dad didn't notice; Mandy could see anything and everything. Life was transparent when she was around; she could see your pain, your hidden fears. He just had to keep her busy when she was home.

Twenty-Three

Matthew and his Dad enjoyed watching old westerns on the new TV; his Mom enjoyed making her first meal in her new kitchen, finally, after cookouts for two evenings and Matthew taking everyone out for breakfast twice. Natalie looked in the den at her two grown men acting like little kids. All she could do was shake her head and laugh. She could see that this was good for Matthew; it was good for Jacob... and her...as well. She worries about Matthew often; he is living in a city that is a huge bulls-eye for terrorist activity, he has no personal life, and he has drifted away from his Godly foundation that he established for himself when he was living at home. She knows that the Word of God says His children are not to worry, but trust in Him; but, as being a parent goes, she will always have 'strong concerns' for Matthew. She doesn't have as much concern for Mandy; she still lives at home, she works in a hospital, and she has a personal relationship with Jesus that many pastors would covet.

Matthew watched the last vacation he had taken with great nostalgia, and with great sorrow. He never realized the unnecessary hidden pain he had caused his parents, especially his Mom. His Dad hid his feelings and emotions much better. It could just be because of Mom's fiery attitude and personality; she kept very few things bottled inside. If she had a question, concern, or an opinion, she was direct and immediate with a response. She never hammered him about his spiritual walk; she always lovingly asked and persuaded. Mandy, however, was another story! She was direct, she was blunt; she always spoke her words kindly and lovingly, but with no regard as to how much it would hurt your feelings. She said that hurt and pain was necessary to grow, to gain knowledge, or become enlightened to a situation you are either unaware of or you are ignoring. Ignorance can kill you. Stubbornness is stupidity. She was full of them; she sounded more like a wife than a sister. God bless the man that falls in love with her! Annoying, yes, at times, but he loved her for her candid honesty. She is what kept him focused, grounded. She kept him from falling farther over the edge after 9/11. He hated to see his vacation end…again. This was the last time he was at home. His only comfort at this moment is in knowing that his gifts were long overdue and greatly appreciated. He even enjoyed the overcooked steaks on the new grill. He had a feeling that they would keep this grill for a while.

Meanwhile, it was a restless night for Mandy, tormented by visions all hours of the night. Each time she would wake up, she would fall to her knees in prayer for her brother. She did not question the inner voice; her spirit knew Matthew was the one who was in turmoil. She never admitted fear; she trusted and believed all of the promises of God throughout His Word, and reminded Him of one of those promises when she prayed.

"Father", Mandy prayed fervently, "You said in Your Word in Mark 11:23 and 24, 'For assuredly, I say to you, whoever says to this mountain, "Be removed and be cast into the sea," and does not doubt in his heart, but believes those things he says will be done, he will have whatever he says.

Therefore I say to you, whatever things you ask when you pray, believe that you will receive them, and you will have them.' And in John 14:13 and 14, You said, 'And whatever you ask in My name, that I will do, that the Father may be glorified in the Son. If you ask anything in My name, I will do it.' Father, I am reminding you of your promise, and I am exercising my right to claim this promise upon the plea I am making now! I do not know what he is going through or what type of attack he is under, but I claim his safety and protection through You! Keep him in Your hand, keep the clutches of the powers of darkness from him! I know You have a purpose for his life; he is just too blind or immature at this time to see it! And now, since I have claimed my rights as a child of God by reminding You of Your promises to me, and I further remind You, as recorded in Isaiah 55:11 that Your Word shall not return to You void! Therefore, I lay this spirit of unrest at Your feet, and declare it settled and my requests fulfilled! I will have peace, and I will rest comfortably the rest of the night! In Jesus' name, Amen!"

Meanwhile back in New York, while Mandy is having her battle with unrest, another person is under a burden of a restless spirit. Elizabeth is praying earnestly for answers. Answers to questions she cannot realize why they are upon her.

"Why am I feeling such unrest, Father? I can sense this is because of Mr. Craig, uh, I mean, Matthew, but why am I being troubled? I only met him last night! Why am I being tormented for him? How can I help him? I shared with him, I listened to him, I offered advice to him; why am I burdened with such an overwhelming desire, no, need, to pray for his safety and well-being? Father, I will listen to your requests, and I will obey and carry out your plan; use me as You need! I trust You with my life, and I will help Matthew anyway You see fit for me to help! Thank you for the peace and understanding that You are sending to me right now! In the name of Jesus, Amen!"

Elizabeth went back to bed with an assurance in her spirit; she was at peace with her petition she took before God. She went back to sleep with no concerns of what her promise might entail; she only knew that she would follow and obey the Lord's wishes. She was still wondering why Matthew was so prevalent in her mind, her thoughts. Despite his inappropriate lifestyle, the drinking, the parties, the women; she could deal with the parties, but what was he looking for? Does he think he will find it by sleeping with every woman he meets? Wait, he said he had only slept with a few... well, that is still being promiscuous! Suddenly, she realized-she was jealous!

"Oh, God, forgive me!" Elizabeth pleaded. "I refuse to lose anymore sleep over him! The unrest I am experiencing now is my fault! He is a very nice man; a very handsome man, I might add, but he is too much maintenance for me to deal with in my life!" She continued arguing with herself, convincing herself that her points were valid points to allow her to dismiss her confused feelings. "I will not allow myself to be involved with someone that does not know the meaning of fidelity! He is not capable of a monogamous relationship! He is not even a Christian! Stop it, Liz! Get a hold of yourself! You will not think anymore of this!"

After saying everything on her mind, she pulled the sheet to her shoulder, rolled over, and began to focus on falling back to sleep. Before falling asleep, a smile formed on her lips; perhaps she was satisfied with her decision, perhaps she was remembering the embrace she shared with Matthew. Regardless, the thought allowed her to return quickly to a peaceful, relaxing sleep.

Matthew was now up to the last two years of his life review. He really did not want to relive it. Despite all the money, fame, popularity, notoriety, and women, he knew the cold and ruthless man he allowed himself to become. He now remembered all of the Sunday morning sermons, all of Mandy's preaching and all of her invitations to accept Jesus as his Lord and Savior. He remembered telling her that he would soon; he was not ready yet. He told himself he could not be the dedicated attorney he needed to be and be the dedicated Christian at a level he felt necessary to be accepted or to be worthy of being considered a Christian. He remembered telling himself that he has given hundreds of thousands of dollars to the rebuilding of new and existing churches, he has given thousands of dollars to various children's and religious charities, as well. He has zealously tried through the legal system to help several that were accused or treated wrongly. He admitted to those that he helped that had wronged others, and apologized for those.

He has never physically murdered anyone, but he could see instances where he has emotionally hurt others. He had killed their hope, their spirit. For that reason, he was guilty of murder. He saw all of the times he had ignored the pleas of his parents to visit, saying he was too busy. He was busy by his choice, not his employer. He could see this was dishonoring his parents. He did not want to count all of the lies; therefore, he moved on to the next subject. He had seen several women in which he would have enjoyed a sexual encounter with them; there were some that actually happened! He was guilty of adultery; his numerous counts of lustful desires would raise the total charges. He told himself that he has never stolen anything in his life; however, when he thought about how he used the law to help in some of his cases, he realized he has indeed been a thief. Sundays were the only day he was not in the office more than a couple of hours. It was his day to physically and mentally relax and recharge. He knew it had been years since he had been to church. He was now guilty of failing to keep the Sabbath day holy. Now, Matthew was not one to curse, but he had seen proof of all the times he had taken the name of God in vain.

Matthew continued to ignore his life replay and continued with his thinking. Is there not a commandment he hasn't broken? He knew God was the creator of all things, Jesus was His son; Jesus died for the sins of the world and returned to life on the third day to prove His defeat of hell and Satan. He considered him The God; all of the others were either false or still very dead or in hell. However, he could see that his cars, his TV, his job, all received more attention than God did; therefore, they would be considered idols. What's left... covetousness? Well, he didn't want anyone's wife, he wanted to own cars like those of some of his colleagues, but he didn't want their car; he did not want to own anyone's home, because he wanted his own place. However, he did want to be as big, no bigger, than some senior partners at his firm were. Would God see that as covetousness?

When he again turned his focus to the screen, he was at a pivotal case in his practice. Of course, he won the case; he made the firm and himself a lot of money, but also one of the cases he wished he had never taken.

For Matthew, it was never about the money; after all, he has given away much more than he has spent for himself. Yes, he collected himself some very nice toys: his cars, top-of-the-line electronics in his home, a very luxurious apart-ment, which he acquired before he was making the absurd amount of money he his now making, and he has invested heavily into his retirement. If he should grow weary and tired of all the nonsense tomorrow, he could pack up and leave the madness behind without blinking twice.

What about the women? Matthew always enjoyed the company of a beautiful woman; however, he never felt a deep sense of longing for any of them. He enjoyed the company of a beautiful woman along side him as he went to all of the business functions, the trendy parties, the award ceremonies, and the charitable events. He never really enjoyed 'the in-crowd' thing, but he never wanted to return to the painfully shy person he was before he had met Pam. The women were always beautiful; most were models, some were hopefuls, and some were hopeless. Some were very intelligent, many were not, but all of them had desire: the desire to be successful, independent, and recognized.

Matthew always enjoyed a good, stimulating conversation along with his dinner; however, those were in short supply, at least with his choice of companions. He realized that the women that could engage in an intelligent conversation excited him as much as the anticipation and the thought of how great the sex was going to be with the woman that was with him. His desire was never more than the satisfaction of a night of hot, animalistic passion. It was all about the sex. It was merely a physical need; it was a way to relieve the stress of the demanding weeks (or possibly months) of a case that he had finally finished. On one occasion, it was to help survive the remainder of a pending case.

Most of his sexual trysts were with those that stimulated him intellectually as well as physically. The ones that didn't, or couldn't, enjoy a conversation that was not all fashion, modeling, and make-up, usually went home after the party. The one that didn't, he considered a mistake. Now, knowing what he knows at this moment, all of them were a mistake. He realized something he thought was rather profound: he had developed an emotional tie to the women that became sexual partners with him; however, he never felt even an inkling of love towards any of them. However, there was respect for them. Some, however, deserved no respect. They were a different class of women all together; they were the few willing to do anything (and with anyone) to reach their goal. He knew the signs to recognize this type, and he stayed clear of them, although, unfortunately, only after having a conversation with two and representing one in court.

As Matthew absorbed the scenes from the last two-plus years of his life, a lot about him and his life had become crystal clear. It was not as successful as he thought it was; he was not as happy as he told himself he was. He was ashamed of himself. He knew how to live; he simply chose to ignore it. After all, he has free will, and he exercised his right to use it. He had plenty of knowledge of who Jesus Christ is; he had his years of church attendance while living at home and he had his sister who lived it every moment of every day. Mandy was a picture of happiness; no, after seeing her again throughout the many scenes in his life, she was joyous! That is what he wanted for himself! But it is too late now. The one last bright spot in his life, strangely enough, is the last day of his life. It was the day he met Elizabeth.

Twenty-Four

He did not know much about her, but he knew more about her from one night of open and honest conversation than he knew about all of the other women in his life over the past five years combined! She was intelligent; he could engage her in a stimulating and challenging conversation. She was confident, passionate about her beliefs, unashamed of her faults and weaknesses, and possibly the most beautiful woman he had ever met. She was not a "glamorous model"; no, Elizabeth's beauty was natural! Her beauty came from within and excreted out of every pore of her body. The minimal amount of makeup she was wearing only hid her true self.

He watched each second with great excitement. He wanted to relive this night repeatedly; not for delaying the inevitable, but to have another opportunity to see her, relive the conversation with her. He had to confess that it was another thing about her that delighted his interest-the conversation. She knew much about current events, she could talk of social issues, she could hold her own in the courtroom, and she was very religious. No, scratch that; that is an insult, a slap in her face. He knew 'religious people.' She was virtuous, committed, dedicated; she was a true Christian in every sense of the word! She was a child of God!

She talked about her relationship with Jesus Christ in a way he had never heard. Mandy had a deep, intimate, personal relationship with Him, and it was evident to anyone and everyone who met her or had a conversation with her. But Elizabeth was at another level; maybe it was because she was not family or maybe it was because she was so breathtakingly beautiful, but it sounded much different to him.

He wished she had been a part of his life sooner; maybe his life would have turned out differently. As he watched the moments of their momentary separation, when he was with Nicole before she departed for her photo opportunity, he was thinking about her. Nicole was too engrossed in her big break to recognize his preoccupation. His good-bye kiss was convincing enough to make her think of things that might be. Although he may have been kissing Nicole, his thoughts were still with Elizabeth. Reliving his life, hearing his thoughts, it was all overwhelming; and when it came to Elizabeth, it was confusing, as well.

He can now see a side of himself that he never seen before. It was similar to the infatuation he once had with Pam, yet it was completely different. Could it be...no, it was too soon to even to think it was love he was feeling. After all, everyone knows that Matthew Craig is incapable of loving. He heard it so many times; he was actually starting to believe it, too. But it still does not change the fact that he was feeling something he has never felt before; could she be the one? Or rather, could she have been the one? There was only drawback to his pointless question. He could afford anything he wanted; he could hire the best people to complete an entire background check on her, he could talk to her more, get to know her better. If given a few more opportunities to be with her, he could determine exactly what he was feeling. He needed the one thing he could not buy – time.

For the last time, he felt the serene, soothing feeling he felt that night he held Elizabeth's hand. And he bathed himself with the warmth, peace, and comfort he felt in their embrace. He felt the excitement once again that he felt when she kissed his cheek. Her lips were as soft as she was! It felt right. He now realizes his last discovery will be that his feelings for Elizabeth were love.

"Mandy was right", Matthew thought aloud. "She always said I was either dead or blind if I couldn't see it." She was referring to the girls that had a crush on him in high school, but if she could, she would have told him the same thing about Elizabeth, except it was he that was transparent this time. Matthew forced a smile and laughed, "It's kind of ironic and prophetic at the same time, huh?"

Matthew began to tremble as he once again looked at the screens. He was now on his way home; he heard the plea he had made to God that night. He again heard the warnings from Mandy in her phone call. He had received several chances; he ignored them all. And as he lay down to sleep that night, he had no idea this ordeal would be the next thing he would experience. He bowed his head in shame…and in fear. He knew, from everything he was taught as a young teenager up until his last night on Earth, this was his eternal fate. His heart was racing, his head was pounding, his body began to convulse uncontrollably.

When the screens faded, a second silhouette now accompanied the brightly glowing silhouette that was there before, appearing on the right hand side of him. The angel that had once accompanied him was now to the right of the second bright silhouette. Matthew knew who, and what, this was.

"Matthew Craig," he heard a powerful, yet very loving voice speak. "I was crucified for you! I went through Hell so you would not have to! I came back here to be at my Father's side to be your intercessor in your time of need. I could have proclaimed you blameless! But you chose to ignore me; you simply rejected every opportunity given to you to become one of my Father's heirs!"

Matthew knew it was the voice of Jesus Christ! He could no longer stand; he crumpled to his knees and hid his face on the ground. "I was such a fool!" he cried. "I have no recourse; I thought I had more time, but then again, I'll bet most everybody thinks that!"

Once again, he heard the thunderous voice of God.

"Now, I ask you, Matthew Craig, how do you plead?" He asked.

"All the evidence speaks for itself!" Matthew admitted. "I have no choice but to say 'guilty'."

He saw the silhouette of Jesus turn to the angel on his right; the angel appeared to be looking for something in a rather large tablet or book of some sort. He saw the angel nod his head negatively. After turning back towards Matthew, He sorrowfully replied, "It breaks my heart, Matthew Craig! After everything I did for you; after giving you several opportunities to repent, you still did not want to accept My gift of eternal life in Heaven!"

Matthew saw the left portion of the screen open to reveal a place unlike any other; it was beyond compare to anything he had ever seen in his life. The grass was greener; the sky was bluer; the water in the nearby stream was clearer. Bright, golden translucent walkways led to a marvelous city that was beyond breathtaking, beyond brilliant. The buildings glistened like diamonds. There were several people there; all were working in unison, young and old alike, and all were singing joyously. No one seemed tired, no one appeared ill. He saw no one wearing glasses or with any other form of handicap. He also noticed that their bodies appeared as if illuminated from within; they were emitting a luminous glow.

"This is what you threw away, Matthew! This could have been your home! You could have been among the eternal joy that they all share!" Jesus said solemnly. "I placed many opportunities in your path, but you chose to continue on your own path, ignoring your warnings of the pending danger. It is not my choice to forbid you from entering into Heaven; for I long to have all of the earth's inhabitants here with Me! You were given free will, free to choose, the path you take while you live your life upon the Earth! Therefore, it is by your choice that you have chosen to live apart from Me and my Father! Since you chose to live for your self, you shall be by your self for eternity! You have chosen to live hellishly; therefore, you have gained access to Hell with the others who chose to live apart from Me and My Word! You will now live in total darkness; not even the flames will be seen! But they will be suffered; they will be felt! They will pierce and penetrate your spirit! The things you experienced on your journey here were nothing! You will be alone with your pain, your suffering, and your regrets! It breaks My heart to say this; good-bye, Matthew Craig, your name is not in the Book of Life! You have been found guilty! Matthew, depart from Me and my Father, and join your master, Satan and his demons in the eternal fire!"

As the doorway to his view of Heaven closed, the other side of the screens opened, allowing a thick, billowing cloud of smoke escape from behind them. The heat that rushed towards him was intense; his fear now at utmost proportions. As the angel pointed him in the direction he was to walk, he began to hear the screams, the wailing; it was similar to the muffled screams he heard at the beginning of this trial, yet it was not even remotely close! He could see others, wrenched into the gargantuan lake of fire. The angels of Heaven could not get close; for they are strictly forbidden from going past the gates. It was Satan's appointed leaders pulling them in, as none of the guilty appears to be going willingly.

Matthew deduced that it would be futile to attempt to avoid the demons; he would only be prolonging the inevitable. He could not define his emotions; words could not accurately describe the terror, the remorse, the finality of this moment. The only way to stop some of the emotions was to face his eternal death as he faced his earthly life. He went all out or not at all. He never backed down from a challenge. Although this was not life, he knew he must face it as he did everything else in life-on his terms. He simply closed his eyes as he took those last steps towards his descent into eternal damnation. The heat was intense; it was hot enough to melt steel yet he remained intact. He almost wished it would destroy him, but he knew that he was going to remain preserved forever, to suffer the torment of the heat. The flames would engulf him but they could not engage him. He thinks Mandy was the one who told him this. When he took his next step, he felt the safety of solid ground betray him. He opened his eyes to see the crimson flames that gradually grow fainter until they become black. This was the reason he closed his eyes to begin with; he wanted to avoid seeing this ghastly panorama. However, human instincts made him open his eyes when his foot felt no ground beneath it, and ultimately his human instincts allowed him to end up here. He closed his eyes again, with the crimson glow on his eyelids as he fell into eternity.

Twenty-Five

It was an unusually bright, red morning sky shining brightly in New York this quiet Sunday morning. The sun was a blazing orange, beginning to burn away any evidence of its crimson beginning. Matthew awakened violently, screaming and flailing his arms and legs as if he were plummeting through the sky. He was thrashing about uncontrollably on his bed, when finally he awakened enough to gain control of his thoughts. He zealously ran his hands over his head and face, methodically moving to his arms, then his torso, and finally his legs. He cautiously examined his surroundings, assuring himself he was in his apartment, his home. He looked at his alarm clock beside his bed; it was only 7:35 AM. He was sweating profusely; he was still envisioning the lucid, graphic images he witnessed in his dream.

How could he witness his entire life replayed in just five hours? Was it a dream? Has it only been five hours since he fell asleep? For all he knew, days, even weeks, could have passed! That would be absurd; he went to his laptop to check his mail as well as to verify the date. Once he realized it was Sunday and he had indeed only been asleep for five hours, he closed his eyes and breathed a heavy sigh of relief. Once reality set in, he fell prone to the floor, crying uncontrollably. His PDA chimed, reminding him of something that was important when he entered it into his calendar. However, it was the least important task he needed to complete right now. He could not stop weeping; he could not move from the floor. His mind was racing with a myriad of emotions.

It took several minutes to regain his composure, and it took longer to regain enough strength to pull himself off the floor. He immediately began searching for the business card Elizabeth had given him last night. He needed to talk to someone; he needed to talk to someone that was in the city. He needed a personal, face-to-face conversation with someone who would understand what he is experiencing. He wasn't sure himself what it is he is experiencing! After a frenzied search, he located her card. He grabbed the phone and hurriedly began dialing. He muttered to himself, "Please, please answer Liz! Please still be at home!"

"Hello, Matthew!" Elizabeth answered in her sweet, polite tone.

Matthew began to talk restlessly, "Oh, thank God you are home! I'm Sorry I'm calling you so early"-

Elizabeth could hear as well as sense the fear he was experiencing. "Matthew, what's wrong? Are you all right?" she asked.

"No, I'm not all right; well, physically, I'm fine. I'm an utter mess mentally and emotionally!" Matthew admitted. "I don't know how to explain it, but I need ... wait I do not want to make you late for church!"

Elizabeth reassured him, "Matt, if something is wrong"-

Matthew interrupted her, "Would you be offended if I invited myself to go to church with you this morning? I really do not want to be alone this morning! I can't quite explain what I'm feeling right now! I feel as if a great weight has lifted from me, but I still feel as if the walls are closing in around me! I know it probably doesn't make sense; I'll tell you everything that happened, I promise! Just please tell me you can do this for me!"

Elizabeth could feel the joy welling up in her spirit; she was also very concerned for Matthew. "Yes, that would be great! But our service begins at 9:45; If you have enough time, you can pick me up at my apartment before we go, or should I just take a taxi and meet you there?"

Matthew responded, "I have two questions: first, where is your church located, and second, how much time do I need? I still need to shower and shave, but I can be at your apartment by 9:20, 9:30 at the latest!"

Elizabeth softly assured him, "That is plenty of time; I'm usually there earlier than that, but"-

"I'm sorry! I don't mean to pull you in to my problems!" Matthew apologized profusely. "It's just I don't know anyone else, I mean, there is over a million people in this city and you are the only person I know that would understand; and I just met you yesterday! Is it possible God planned it this way?"

Elizabeth, stunned by his question, was temporarily speechless. Is this the same man, who just twelve hours ago, was trying to understand her love and her commitment to Jesus Christ and His Word? She now knew that whatever happened was supernatural, it was only something that could have been wrought by God. "God does work in mysterious ways, Matt!" she replied. "Anything is possible with God!"

I've got to go!" Matthew exclaimed. "I'll never get there in time! By the way, where are we going to church?"

"Oh yes, that info might be helpful! We are going to Kingdom Fellowship! It's a little drive; it is over on the East side on 143rd Street!" Elizabeth announced. "I'll see you in a little while!"

Matthew carefully but hurriedly shaved while he was in the shower. He quickly dried off, combed his hair, and walked into his closet. He did not know what would be the proper dress for this church. Would it matter, rather, should it matter? He grabbed one of his casual business suits, sans tie, and walked back into the bedroom. After getting dressed, he looked at the man staring back at him; he appeared to be a rather neat, organized fellow, especially in comparison to the much-disheveled shell of a man that he was just over an hour ago! He stared for what seemed like minutes but was only seconds. He turned and quickly headed towards the living room. He grabbed his car keys and Elizabeth's business card to remember her address and headed out the door.

Traffic was unusually light on this morning; Matthew was saying, "Thank you, God! Thank you, God!" the entire drive to Elizabeth's apartment. When he pulled in front of her building, the security guard notified Miss Angel that her transportation was waiting at the door.

When Elizabeth appeared at the doorway, Matthew forgot everything for a moment. She was even more stunning than the night before! The white cotton dress, adorned with a beautiful amethyst colored flower, looked as if made especially for her. Her hair draped over her shoulders, and bounced in rhythm to her steps. She got into the car and smiled quizzically at Matthew. "Good morning, Matthew! You certainly look better than you sounded on the phone earlier!" she announced.

"You get the credit for that," Matthew revealed, his voice still quivering. "Thank you for everything! I have no right to impose this upon you, but I did not want to go to church alone; I did not want to be surrounded by strangers! I need to know at least one face in the crowd! And, if I should need it, someone who can give me a word of encouragement, a hand on my shoulder; you know, offer support when I need it!"

Elizabeth was moved by his open display of emotions. Before she could ask him to elaborate, they were at the church. Once Matthew parked the car, he quickly ran around to Elizabeth's side of the car to open her door and offer his hand to assist her in getting out of the car. He was at her mercy, as he did not know where to go. He discreetly cradled her arm inside his and allowed her to direct him to the inside of the sanctuary.

The church was located inside an old Victorian-style building, quite possibly one of the old eighteenth century houses that meticulously preserved and restored throughout the years. There were no stained-glass windows; however, the cracked-glass pattern allowed prisms of light to emanate upon various chairs in the sanctuary. The area behind the pulpit and the altar were extraordinary! There were acoustic guitars, electric guitars, bass guitars, drums, saxophones, keyboards, and violins! Matthew had never seen or heard 'church music' played with so many different instruments!

Matthew was still absorbing the beauty and the tranquility of the sanctuary when several people began walking up and began talking with Elizabeth. She graciously and respectfully introduced Matthew, informing them he was an attorney, who has helped several people with nowhere else to turn. Everyone was sincere, open, and very friendly! They eagerly but warmly reached out to shake his hand, welcoming him to their church. He could sense their affection and outpouring of interest was genuine; he had never experienced this since he was still attending church back in New Hope!

When the band began to play, the place became silent. The music was unlike anything he ever heard in church before, or anywhere else for that matter! The songs were not 'dried up'; it was not the old, traditional, and, although still a vital part of many churches, somewhat worn songs of yesteryear. Each of the songs had a message, and each message was different: humility, deliverance, reverence, love, honor, and praise. The music relaxed him somewhat; he could feel the tension melting from his neck and shoulders. Elizabeth noticed it, too. She smiled after glancing at him and seeing his stature return to what she remembered from just last night.

Matthew did not know if it was proper, correct, or allowed. He could not wait until after the service; he needed to repent and confess now! He turned to Elizabeth, "Liz, I can't wait!" he whispered. "I need to go up there, now!"

Elizabeth nodded approvingly as she smiled and squeezed his hand.

It felt as if he ran there; he probably looked desperate, even crazy. He really didn't care what others thought. He needed to thank his Creator for giving him another chance! He needed to beg forgiveness from the One who died on a cross for his transgressions; he needed to repent of his sinful, worldly way of living to Jesus! He continued talking, confessing, crying, and even laughing on an occasion, for what seemed like forever. About halfway through his plea for forgiveness, he felt a soft, warm hand resting on his shoulder. It was comforting; it encouraged and strengthened him. It allowed him to defeat the attack of negativity and discouragement in which the enemy was attempting to derail him. He noticed at some point that the singing had stopped; only the beautiful, melodic music continued.

When he finished, he removed his handkerchief to dry his eyes and cheeks before standing up. Once he did stand to return to his seat, it was then he saw whose hand was on his shoulder. It was Elizabeth; there were at least another 40-50 people standing around him! God had put a gauntlet of warriors around him to fend off the arrows the enemy attempted to deliver.

Elizabeth reached out to hug Matthew; and as he embraced her, he whispered softly in her ear, "Thank you for everything!" Everyone wanted to either hug him or shake his hand; no one was judgmental, no one questioned his sincerity, and no one seemed to care what he had done in the past. There was no murmuring or whispering other than many wanting to know the name of the new man in God's family.

The pastor was the last of those to hug and welcome him into the adopted family of believers. The message was short; the pastor announced that the Holy Spirit had other plans today, and although he sensed in his spirit that something was going to take place today, he did not know what it would be. Now he knows.

The hugs and handshakes continued after the service ended, and did not end until seemingly every person that was there today had congratulated him. Matthew walked Elizabeth back to his car. Along the way he asked, "Would I be imposing upon you too much if I were to invite you to lunch? I'm not ready to go home, and I feel I owe you an explanation!"

Elizabeth jokingly replied, "As long as you take me someplace expensive!"

"You name the place, and I'll drive!" Matthew agreed, not realizing the banter of her request.

"Anywhere you choose is fine." Elizabeth softly replied.

Matthew drove them to an exquisite restaurant on West Broadway. Luckily, they did not need a reservation, as it was a slow Sunday. The hostess led them to a corner table and took their drink orders. While waiting on their iced tea and a Pepsi, Matthew began to tell her about the night before. He told her about Mandy's phone call and the things she had said to him.

When their drinks arrived, they were ready to order. They both quickly gave their requests and Matthew continued with his detailed recollection. He told her about waking up to find the building and then the city in total darkness. He explained how neither his landline phone nor his cell phone worked.

Then he proceeded to tell her about his blind journey through what he thought was his building.

They served their appetizers about the time when Matthew began smelling smoke, and by the time their main course arrived, he was at the point where he could smell what at that time was burning flesh. As Matthew continued telling of his hellish nightmare, Elizabeth's appearance reflected what he was saying; she expressed a gamut of emotions: anxiety, concern, anticipation, fear, shock, depression, anticipation, happiness, panic, and finally terror. Neither was aware of anyone or anything else around them. He desperately needed to share his dream, and she was a very devoted listener. He was still revealing graphic details of his ordeal when they cleared the dishes from their table. Matthew had reached the end of his tale of his trial as they finished off the last of their many refills.

As they were walking back to the car, Matthew implored, "Would it be too much to ask for your help if I were to need assistance this week in locating a Christian bookstore? I am going to need to buy a few things to help me in this new life! You know, this means we are going to be seeing each other a lot more often!"

Just before getting in the car, Elizabeth chuckled, "It may cost you another meal! But, let's get a pizza next time, if that's okay with you!"

Matthew smiled joyfully. "As long as we get extra cheese!" he said, as he closed her door. He was looking forward to their shopping date, as well as learning more about her while he grew more in Christ.

He was also looking forward to getting additional help in his faith walk from his best friend in the world; as soon as he returned home, he needed to call Mandy.

"Finally!" he could already hear her say. This caused him to chuckle as he got into the car.

"Is something wrong?" Elizabeth asked with concern.

"No, nothing is wrong! For the first time, everything is right!" Matthew replied, as they drove off towards home, with the sun shining brightly above them, and shining brightly within them.

Printed in the United States
99113LV00001B/217-228/A

9 781604 770797